To all the readers of Saturday Special
who have shared my joys and sorrows.

SATURDAY VERY SPECIAL!

Even more joys of everyday living

By
BETTY BROOKE

In aid of
Jersey Hospice Care

First edition 2004
© Betty Brooke

ISBN 1-905095-00-7

Cover design by Al Thomas
Typesetting by Rob Shipley

CONTENTS

FOREWORD

Saturday Special and Saturday Extra Special were published as collections of my weekly column in the Jersey Evening Post in 1987 and 1989. The column has been published every week since 1962 and many readers have asked for a third edition so that they can have a permanent record of the articles. I have always been moved by readers who produce from a wallet or a handbag a yellowed Saturday Special which they had cut out years ago when they had found courage or help from something which I had written.

This new collection has a special purpose for it is being sold in aid of Jersey Hospice Care, an organisation which does so much for those facing the problems of serious illness. As I wanted all the proceeds to go to Hospice I did not go to a publishers but asked a colleague, Rob Shipley, to help me put the book together. I also prevailed upon artist and cartoonist Al Thomas, who produced the covers and illustrations for the first two collections, to use his skills once more. Both Rob and Al donated their time and expertise freely for Hospice.

I must also thank the Jersey Evening Post for generously giving permission for material from my column to be reproduced.

DEARLY BELOVED, LET US BRAY

THE donkey and I looked at each other for a few awkward minutes. I had the advantage, standing on the top of the small flight of stone steps leading into the church. He, on the other hand, was at street level and somewhat reluctant to mount the steps accompanied by a band of children. To the side of the steps there was a ramp for wheelchair access, and it was thought by the man who was leading him that the donkey might prefer to join the disabled for a few moments.

Once up the ramp, the donkey stopped in his tracks to allow a boy to get on his back prior to his 'triumphal entry' into the church. Both had important roles on Palm Sunday, and as my experience of donkeys has not, on the whole, been good. I hoped that he would be willing to process down the church aisle after me.

I ought perhaps at this stage to mention that most of the donkeys I knew in Malta, where I lived for four years, were not very co-operative. They also had a raucous laugh when they were disobeying an order which made one feel discomfited.

I hoped that this donkey, who was looking reluctant to enter the church door, would not indulge in one of the donkey brays which would electrify the waiting congregation. I need have had no fear. He was a very civilised donkey, but he was not an enthusiastic worshipper. His owner was, however, wise in the ways of donkeys, and produced from his pocket a pack of Polo mints. The donkey chewed one reflectively.

We processed down the aisle with the donkey being slipped Polo mints at regular intervals. When we got to the front of the church, he burped gently and a little spittle fell on to the blue carpet. I caught his eye. Was that a wink?

His departure was without incident, and for a few moments the congregation had been transported back to the scene of Jesus entering Jerusalem on the back of a donkey. The Bible refers to it as The Triumphal Entry.

Remembering the incident, I found myself thinking that the old expression that a carrot is better than a stick for an obstinate donkey has great truth. Most of us can be persuaded to be more co-operative if there is a reward rather than a punishment at the end of the road. At the risk of once more being accused of flippancy, perhaps I could end with an adaptation of the old proverb.

Fine words may butter no parsnips, but a mint with a hole in the centre can move even a reluctant donkey.

KEEPING IN TOUCH WITH GOD

'YOU must he using the phone when I'm out', I said to Tovey, the black dog with the Queen Anne legs who shares my life. 'After all,' I continued, 'I live alone except for you and this quarter's phone bill is appalling.'

The fact that it came two days before Christmas did not make it any easier to bear. Somehow the spirit of goodwill was somewhat diminished when I opened it, and filing the receipt has reminded me of the shock.

Tovey looked at me in the unblinking way of dog who suspects his mistress is losing what remains of her mind.

Our conversations over the years have been many. I am by nature a communicator and when there is no person around with whom to exchange the pearls of wisdom and the problems of the day, Tovey has perforce to be the sounding board for my ideas and complaints. He has never to date contributed greatly to our everyday exchanges. I always bid him good morning and good night, and he wags his tail in acknowledgement of these pleasantries. His conversation is limited to informing me loudly and vociferously if there is someone at the cottage door, a rabbit crossing a field half a vergée away, or a bird taking off in the shrubbery. His voice is not attractive – he has a curiously, loud unmelodic bark and it has a quality of insistence which makes action imperative. If he could physically propel me to the front door to let a caller in he would do it. However, he has to confine himself to rushing to wherever I am and making a series of circles around me get me to go the door.

In the matter of distant rabbits his action is different. He leaps to his feet, rising spectacularly out of his basket and causing me to have a minor heart flutter, fearing that there is a burglar in the vicinity. Thereafter he leaps at the door to get out to patrol the garden until the distant rabbit disappears.

Tovey is not a quite biddable dog. He is a noisy dog who enjoys participating in everything that is happening. If he were human he would be a political activist with militant tendencies.

Perhaps I have wandered a long way from the telephone account which sparked off this Saturday Special. There is, of course, a connection, for my phone is my lifeline to those whom I cannot always meet and as long as I can pay the bill the telephone is worth every penny to me as a means of communication. After all, there is a limit to Tovey's conversational abilities! It is good to keep in regular touch with friends and with our Father in heaven.

It's better to say a prayer every day than make an emergency call in a crisis.

10

AS THE SANDS OF TIME RUN DOWN . . .

LAST month I had to renew the flat roof of my cottage. This may not seem a major piece of work, but the cottage at the top of the valley is deceptive in its roof area.

It does not look, at first glance, like a house with a vast area of flat roof, but there is a very large area covered with roofing material and it is 15 years since it was re-felted.

One of the interesting aspects of getting work done nowadays is to realise that, as I have mentioned in this column before, 'a lifetime's guarantee' is not something that I really need any more.

I have not the whole of a lifetime left, so the 15-year guarantee is quite adequate. Even as I write this, I realise that the sand is definitely further down life's egg-timer than it was.

There was a time when the bottom half of the egg-timer did not contain too much sand, but now the top half looks less full than I really like.

I cannot think where the years have gone: it seems only yesterday that I was looking in the mirror and worrying because I could see a white hair.

Now when I look in the mirror I have great difficulty seeing a dark lock! My eyebrows are not yet white, although Tovey, the dog with the Queen Anne legs who shares my life, has now pure white eyebrows. I have to own that I preferred us both when we looked more obviously youthful.

It is a fact of life that time passes very slowly when we are young; it is an eternity to the summer holidays and freedom from school. Waiting for a birthday, with its party and presents, used to seem like forever, but now they come around with alarming frequency.

I am often asked if I would like to turn the clock back and start all over again. I have to admit that such a prospect would not thrill me with delight, although I have had an enormously happy life. The dark days have been many it is true, but the sunny days have been memorable and what is nowadays called 'life's rich tapestry' has been for me a canvas much enhanced by the loves and friendships which have so enriched my life.

Strange that re-felting the roof has made me think of time past and present. I hope that I may after 15 years have the roof once more re-felted. I will be quite young enough still to see that the work is put in hand!

God grant me strength for each
day and friends to companion
me every step of the way.

IT TAKES ONLY TWO MINUTES

TWO minutes of silence can seem an eternity to those people for whom silence is a totally unknown and unlovable experience.

They live in a world of blaring radio programmes or with rooms papered with wall to-wall television. Silence is somehow a threatening experience and those who try to, shut it out with every sort of device.

On 11 November 1918 peace was declared in that war which historians are wont to call the Great War. It was certainly 'Great' if one measured it by the casualty lists which made such gruesome reading for those alive at the time.

It was a war in which troops were massacred in the trenches and where many of the men on both sides of No Man's Land had little idea of why they were killing each other.

The idea of honouring those who died with a period of two minutes' silence stems from that war and has encompassed those who were casualties in the wars that have taken place since. It is little enough for those of us who owe our freedom to the sacrifices of so many to stop and, in silence, remember them.

Why then are there those who are resistant to the idea of observing a period of respect for the dead? Is it merely the discomfort of the silence when just for two minutes out of a 24 hour day one is forced to stop and think or pray and pay homage to the dead?

I do not know the answer to the questions that I pose but, if it is that memories are short, then I believe they should be jogged.

Or is it that we should not expect those who knew nothing of war to remember those who died or who were permanently injured? I cannot believe this to be the case.

We must educate our young people to realise what has been done on their behalf and we must remind the middle-aged who escaped being killed that there is a time for remembrance and gratitude. I have stood with other members of the forces around cenotaphs in many places and felt the cold chill or the soaking rain failing on our uniformed ranks.

I have watched wreaths being laid as the 'Last Post' was sounded by a solitary bugler. I have never failed to find the tears welling in my eyes as I remembered friends who died. I will not grudge them two minutes of my thoughts.

> *At the going down of the sun and in the*
> *morning we will remember them.*

> Binyon

LIGHTNING STRIKES ON A LEVEL FIELD

WHEN all the lights went out earlier this month and I groped about in the darkness to find a match to light the candle which sits ready for just such an emergency I found myself wondering what had caused the power failure.

Looking out of the cottage window I could see that I was not alone in the dark. Turning on BBC Radio Jersey I heard that the cause of the trouble was a lightning strike in France and I muttered some words under my breath about the irresponsible Electricité de France employees.

The next morning, I discovered I had misjudged our brothers across the water. One of their power stations on the French coast had been hit by lightning, and my assumption that a lightning strike meant sudden industrial action was quite wrong.

Lightning strikes, like wild-cat strikes, have crept into our language and do not necessarily mean what they seem at first glance. Wild-cat strikes are not feral pussies on the rampage lashing out at passersby. They take place when workers down tools without the blessing of their union.

As I was pondering along these lines I thought of other phrases which are in everyday use but do not actually mean what the phrase may suggest.

When we hear of someone shooting himself or herself in the foot this does not mean there are any firearms involved in the exercise. It is used to denote making a bloomer or scoring an own goal. Originally I thought the phrase to shoot oneself in the foot meant to try to get a Blighty ticket in the First World War. However, that meaning has gone and only the older generation would know what a Blighty ticket represented.

For those suffering the horrors of constant shellfire in the trench warfare of 1914-1918 an undetected self-inflicted wound might well get the posting back home which was so attractive.

Today, scarcely a day passes without reading, when negotiations are taking place, the phrase 'a level playing field'. Everyone wants a level playing field so that in negotiations there is a sense of equality.

I was given a little book as an extra present this Christmas entitled 'Gentle Thoughts'. It is full of wise sayings and there is a phrase in it which cannot be misunderstood.

> *It is important that people know what you stand for.*
> *It's equally important that they know what you*
> *won't stand for.*

Mary Waldrop

THE COMFORT OF NIGHT-TIME COMPANIONS

'I REALLY miss him lying there in the night,' said the voice at the other end of the telephone. 'I know what you mean,' I replied. 'He's a sort of comforting presence.'

Lest there are readers who are already pricking up their ears and murmuring to themselves about a romance which is about to be unfolded, let me disabuse them at the outset. The reference to a 'comforting presence' was that of a black dog with Queen Anne legs who has his bed carried into my bedroom and shares the night watches with me.

I have been on holiday for the past three weeks so that my cottage-sitter found herself perforce sharing my downstairs bedroom with a canine companion. My cottage-sitter had at first expressed some concern about Tovey as a companion of the night.

However, I assured her that he did not snore, never moved and alerted me only if there were something untoward happening in the vicinity. As Tovey in the evening of his life goes to bed at 8 pm and starts to drag his bed into my room at that hour, one is made aware that his day is ending whatever the person who shares the room intends to do.

I alerted the cottage-sitter of this new habit and I gathered that my absence did not mean that he sat at the sitting room window all evening awaiting my return. He realised that he was once more deserted and made the best of the situation.

I have spoken to many people who, over the years, have lost a lifetime human companion. For many, the loneliness of the night hours is the worst. There is no one there to whom one can reach out a hand and share the worrying contents of a bad dream. Loneliness is particularly hard to bear at night.

During the day one can busy oneself about daily chores, and daylight hours are never so frightening. It is when darkness falls that fears return and being alone becomes something which has to be endured.

Having slept on my own for nearly 30 years I am an authority on the subject of occasionally wishing the night would pass. In a book by Phil Bosmans in a section headlined 'Comfort' there are these lines:

> *Comfort is the gentle face of someone close to you, who understands your tears, who listens to your troubled thoughts, who sticks by you through your doubts and anxieties, and who shows you a few guiding stars in the dark night.*

McBROOKE'S TAKEAWAY

MY blackbird has got bored with patronising the takeaway food business and has decided to bring the youngsters to the restaurant to eat.

For some time she had been engaged in carrying food from the bird table outside my kitchen window to the family at home. This has been an exhausting business for her and on Sunday this week I witnessed the first family outing to McBrooke's, the Rozel Fast Food Café.

The restaurant is immediately outside my kitchen window and on a level with it. This gives the customers a bird's eye view of me breakfasting, and allows me to see them enjoying the food which I provide.

It was a very special delight to see Mother Blackbird fly in, closely followed by her three fledglings, who were going to have their first eating-out experience. The three youngsters were a bit unsteady on their wings, but they sat firmly on the table and waited for mother to stuff crumbs into their open beaks.

She tried to show them that all they had to do was put their beaks on the table and scoop up the crumbs as she was doing. They were, in educational terms, slow learners. They stood open-beaked, waiting.

Eventually, like mothers since time began, she gave in for the sake of peace. She fed them and I watched. It was a rare privilege. The family returned to McBrooke's the next morning and once more mother fed her young at the table.

On Tuesday she ignored their cries, and first one and then the other bent down and pecked at the crumbs. Eating out had become acceptable.

From the time when a child is weaned until the day the young adult leaves home, mothers and fathers have an enormous responsibility. They have to draw a fine line between teaching children to be independent and at the same time giving them the security which is such an important part of family life.

At this time of the year parents are anticipating their sons and daughters making plans to leave home for college or for job opportunities. The house which once rang with the voices of young people and their friends will be silent. No longer will it be necessary to go on mug hunts to find the coffee receptacles which somehow get strewn around the house like so many paperchase clues.

It is a time of transition for families and just as my blackbird family suddenly became independent, so it is for many families at this time as they contemplate a different pattern of family life.

In a book of prayers I found this under the Family Life section:

Thank you for the different steps of family life;
Being cared for as a child;
Growing up and discovering ourselves;
Breaking free and living our own lives;
Finding the miracle of someone else's love;
Bringing new life into the world;
Caring for children and watching them grow;
Father of all families, thank you for our family.

SLEEP THE SLEEP OF THE UNTROUBLED

I NOW have a telephone which incorporates a radio, a clock and an alarm. I am aware, even as I write of this new toy, that there are those who will sniff and say that there is nothing special about such technology but for me it seems to be remarkable that so much can be contained in one instrument.

The purchase of this equipment from our merry men at Telephone House was not undertaken by me lightly. Those who know me well would be witness to the fact that, generally speaking, I am a canny Scot despite having lived here for nearly 40 years.

There have always been the impulsive moments when I have strayed from the path of thrift, which is my familiar route, but on the whole I do not wander much onto the road of extravagance which leads to disaster.

I had to have a new telephone because mine had become faulty. I had also to accept that the radio which is my lifeline in my bedroom had been knocked so often off the bedside table that it was in a fragile state of health. As for the alarm clock, I have to own that its bell does not ring at all if one forgets to wind it up! So the possibility of a telephone combining all these features was irresistible.

I had difficulty during the first night finding the switches that I needed to cope with the radio. I had become so used to putting my hand out and knocking the old friend flat on its face that the more stable replacement was strange at first. The clock has large lighted-up digital numbers which tell the time and there is, fortunately as I discovered as I lay bathed in light, a switch which dims this dial. How thoughtful of the maker to realise that those of us who are past the age of night lights are still made to feel uneasy by the shadows cast by the bedside chair on the ceiling.

I came across an evening prayer last week which I think is good to say when we are anxious and troubled:

Give me sound and refreshing sleep;

16

Give me safety from all perils;
Give, me in my sleep freedom from restless dreams;
Give me control of my thoughts if I should lie awake;
Give me wisdom to remember that night was made for
sleeping and not for the harbouring of anxious of shameful
thoughts.
Give me grace, as I lie abed to think upon thee.

MAD CAR DISEASE

LAST week I was sitting in the garden of my cottage, enjoying a cup of tea with a friend, when a gentle moan came from her car, which was sitting in the drive.

It was the sort of sound which a cow with laryngitis would make or a foghorn makes when it is running short of power.

I decided I must be hearing things, as my coffee-drinking friend, who has acute hearing, took no notice.

A short while afterwards there was another gentle wail from the car. It sounded exactly like a car keening for some departed love.

'Your car is moaning to itself,' I said casually, hoping that I was not the only one hearing the sound.

'It does that,' she said. 'I don't know why.

We returned to our conversation, which was punctuated at intervals by moans from the little Japanese number holding its own wake.

The next day as I passed my car in the garage, it groaned audibly. The gentle moaning continued throughout the afternoon at quite long intervals.

A friend who heard it told me that it must be Mad Car Disease, and I wondered if mine had caught it from the one which had parked the day before in the drive. If it were an infection, I argued, it had taken 24 hours to incubate.

I was glad that the trouble had not begun the day before. Having two products from the Land of the Rising Sun moaning in unison would have been more than I could have borne.

I would be glad to know the cause of this phenomenon. Is it the hot weather which has caused the petrol to expand, and is this keening an escape valve mechanism?

I hesitate to go to the garage, because it will not do it to order. Although not sensitive to ridicule, I cannot imagine how I would describe my problem to the mechanic.

Every part of life nowadays seems fraught with problems.

If sausages are now suspect, goodness knows what the pundits

17

are going to say about haggis!

On a more serious note this week, I have been concerned – as have other thinking people – about the problems which the beef industry is facing. The action by education authorities in taking beef off school menus has been criticised by those who believe that such action is precipitate.

Decisions are never easy to make, and I would merely mention a precept which is attributed to Gypsy Smith.

> *It is better to build a fence around the top of the precipice before a child goes over it than it is to build a hospital at the bottom.*

A SENSE OF ADVENTURE

NO ONE could say that Tovey, the black dog with Queen Anne legs who shares my life, is a gourmet. Nouvelle cuisine and all the rich sauces and esoteric cookery extravagances would be absolutely lost on him. His diet is extremely simple; he has a drink of milk for breakfast and a bone-shaped dog biscuit. He eats his main meal at 5 o'clock and this never varies. He always has the same tinned dog food and any leftover vegetables. That is mixed up with dog meal and he has always finished and is licking the dish before I can get out of the kitchen.

He knows when it is five o'clock and his excitement every afternoon is wonderful to see. On the rare occasions when I have given him some leftover 'people food', he eats it and then sits by his dish waiting for what he considers is his proper meal.

Tovey could be described as a traditionalist when it comes to food. Any departure from the norm he views with grave distrust and eats only what is the alternative with marked reluctance.

I have known some children whose taste is as conservative as Tovey's. Fish fingers and sausages are for them their staple diet and any suggestions that that there are more exciting culinary delights they view with suspicion. 'I won't like it,' they say defiantly when some new dish is suggested and, faced with such a preconceived notion, most parents accept defeat.

So often in life we, who are older, are reluctant to try new ideas. We prefer the old familiar ways because they are the well loved and well known paths. However, in our journey through life, whether it be our inner spiritual journey or our ordinary everyday living, we sometimes have to take our courage in both hands and launch into the unfamiliar waters.

Help me God to launch out into the deep secure in the knowledge that You will be with me and will support me.

DON'T STRIVE FOR THE IMPOSSIBLE

ONE of my lifelong ambitions has been fulfilled. It was not a major ambition but one which I had at the back of my mind for a long time. I had always wanted to ride on a camel. I had not spoken of this secret desire to anyone for I did not really want to witness the quickly hidden smile and the look of disbelief on the faces of those whom I knew well.

However, my ambition was achieved on 18 January 1992 when I climbed off the camel and patted him in a possessive way. Fortunately he had a home-made muzzle on or I might have come back from Tunisia minus a hand.

The trip to Hammamet was not planned for I was in London spending a twenty-day break after my seven-week break!

My readers, who follow this column with varying degrees of interest, will know exactly what I mean by the seven-week break – which involved an arm.

Unplastered and ready for anything, I went into a travel agent and was tempted by a very cheap seven-day package holiday by scheduled flight to a four-star hotel. What tempted me was not only the cheapness of the holiday – although that was a major attraction – but also the fact that there was a picture of a camel on one of the posters.

As the tour agent spoke of the heated swimming pool, the belly dancers who appeared nightly in the cabaret and the Moorish bath, which was apparently even better than the Turkish variety, my eyes were steadfastly fixed on the camel.

Six days later I stood on the hotel balcony and viewed the line of camels outside on the edge of the Mediterranean. I could scarcely wait for the moment to come when I would get aboard a ship of the desert and fulfil my ambition.

It was even better than I had imagined. True, the descent when the camel knelt to let me off was a rather dramatic moment. He was a very tall camel and it was only the prospect of returning with a plastered neck that made me cling on with great intensity.

I had achieved my ambition and I have to say it came up to expectation. I think in life it is perhaps sensible to match your ambitions to what is achievable. I have never hankered after the impossible, which is perhaps why I am on the whole a contented person.

St Thomas More sums up my philosophy very neatly.

The things good Lord, that I pray for, give me grace to labour for.

MYSTERIES MADE BY MACHINES

'IF I had the strength and the windows were not double-glazed, I would throw the whole boiling through the window,' I said to Simon, who has had to put up with being part of a one-parent family since his beloved father died.

Like most single mothers, I have tried to encompass the skills of both parents. There have been times when, I imagine, I have succeeded and other times when I have been a lamentable failure – but then how many mothers, whether single, married or with a partner, would not agree with that statement?

Of course when one's offspring grows to adulthood, and in some cases to maturity, there comes a role reversal when the parent becomes dependent on the child she or he once reared.

This became very apparent to me after 12 January. It was not a significant date in my personal calendar. I did not suffer a physical or mental breakdown on that day in January. It was simply the date on which I bought the computer at which I am sitting writing this article.

That purchase, which was meant to take me into the wonderful world of e-mail, the web and the like, has reduced me from being a semi-competent person to a blithering idiot.

I will not go into details about the articles I have lost, the ones I have filed in totally the wrong folder or the e-mails which have utterly refused to leave the out box and go over the airways to some distant recipient. It is bad enough being a failure, but to have the machine with its screen spitting out messages to me underlining my incompetence is soul-destroying.

The other week it printed in big letters FAILURE and threatened me with all sorts of disasters if I did not do exactly as it told me. I tried but did not succeed!

Everyone has done their best to help me get familiar with this monster on my desk in the Granary – Upstairs Clare, down-the-road-Charlie, across-the-road Peter and long-suffering Simon have all put matters right and reassured me that it is not that I am a fool, but that I do not always take notice of what the machine is telling me to do.

I am really trying harder and asking God to forgive my impatience and my stupidity. The trouble is that I have no one to blame for my failures until this week, when I found this wonderful quotation.

To err is human, but to really foul things up requires a computer.

Farmers Weekly, 1978

TAKING A LITTLE LESS FOR GRANTED

'SI TU prends ma place, prends aussi mon handicap.' Seeing these words of warning written on a notice in a disabled bay in a French town made me think that it was a good way of warning those who parked illegally to think what they were doing.

As someone who has had a disabled parking badge for some years now, I know how irritating it is to find all the spaces occupied and some illegally by those drivers who are hale and hearty and quite able to walk to a multi-storey car park or to a non-disabled parking area. Some of us do not look disabled. We may not have a stick or crutches or a zimmer frame but are nevertheless thought by our doctors in need of special parking.

I was questioned recently by a passer-by jealous of *my* parking space, who said: 'Lucky you, having a disabled badge.'

'You can have my badge if you take my lungs as well,' I said brightly.

Emphysema is a slight handicap to my way of living and is as nothing compared with what many disabled people suffer, but it does limit my ability to walk very far, to move at speed or to tackle any but the slightest incline. I am greatly blessed, as are fellow asthmatics and other emphysema sufferers, by lung-relieving puffers and each morning I link up to my nebuliser and then jump out of bed with a will.

It is a strange thing that one never really appreciates in life certain things until one loses them. I never thought about breathing when my lungs were adequate for most of the tasks I asked them to perform. In the same way, of course, one does not always appreciate friends and relations until they are no longer with us. We take so many things and so many people for granted. We expect them always to be there for us and when suddenly they are taken away and we have to face life without their companionship there can be a dreadful gap.

Naturally, one does not miss those who were not particularly dear to us. Their passing does not diminish us as does the loss of a loved one. Death does not just take human love out of our lives – I have one friend who lost her beloved cat a little while ago but now there is a cat-shaped gap in her life which will never be filled.

As God loves you, thank Him everyday for those
Whom you loved and lost and for those
Whom you still love and who love you.

THE CHAINS OF RESPONSIBILITY

'THERE is absolutely no need at all for you to sit looking at my suitcase as if you are to be abandoned. Indeed, you have what the social services pundits call a vast network of carers, walkers, feeders and people to assume responsibility for you when I am away.'

This conversation took place when Tovey, the black dog with the Queen Anne legs, who shares my life, discovered that my suitcase had appeared and he went instantly into what the vet would describe, I am sure, as a clinical depression. I normally leave the packing until the last minute to avoid this scene when Tovey manages, at the least sight of the case, to give me an enormous guilt complex.

I did not exaggerate when I spoke about his network of carers. Not only does a namesake of mine move over from London to enjoy a holiday in the cottage, with the added responsibility of keeping him company, but Upstairs Rachel, my Depend-upon-Dulcie, plus his regular Sunday walkers, Reg and Jean, are all dedicated to his welfare. Yet he manages with his downcast tail and baleful looks to make me feel that I should never desert him. I was told that for a few days after I had gone on holiday his depression was evident.

But it does not put him off his food, for only a direct hit on the cottage with a bomb would prevent him licking his dish clean.

At this time of the year, when people are planning to go away, there are those with much greater responsibilities than mine who find that the effort is hardly worth the pleasure. Small children, like some wines, do not always travel well. Those who have the responsibility of caring for elderly relatives, and I had such a period in my life, know how difficult it is to ensure the happiness and well-being of those who have to stay at home. Workaholics who cannot bear to leave their offices and who are, like Siamese twins, permanently linked to their mobile phones are often poor travelling companions.

Work and relationships do make demands on our lives, but we must never allow them to absorb us so that we begin to feel indispensable.

Help me God to let go sometimes so that I can recharge my batteries by sitting in the sun and thinking of non-earthly things.

DRIVEN TO DISTRACTION

ALTHOUGH the tourist season is not yet really at its height and the powers that be are not too sure if it will ever reach the record figures of the old days, the traffic seems in summer to get more tiresome than ever.

In the winter there are the Roads Festivals, when we celebrate by having some vital road dug up and there are delays and diversions. When summer comes the digging ceases and the H-cars proliferate.

There was some word from those ever anxious to defend us from any sort of discrimination of taking car hire operators to the Court of Human Rights for putting the letter H on these vehicles which they rent out. Apparently, there are those who hire cars who might feel some sort of discrimination and even persecution because the letter H makes them different from other drivers. I think it is a great advantage to be seen to be a stranger on our shores, for surely we are more careful to avoid them and more willing to give traffic directions and the like to H-car users.

I was asked recently by a reader if I could supply the last two lines to a poem entitled Prayer of a Poor Pedestrian. After some searching, the clue that there was an account of the Prince of Wales's wedding gift on the back of the cutting containing the prayer helped us to trace it to 25 July 1981. It seemed so appropriate that I thought I would use it again.

Prayer of a Poor Pedestrian

O God who filled all heaven with stars,
And then all earth with motor cars,
Make room within Thy cosmic plan
For me, a poor pedestrian.

Spread Thou before me I entreat,
A threadlike pathway for my feet;
And do Thou watch me lest I stray
From this, Thy straight and narrow way.

Give me an ear alert, acute,
For each swift car's peremptory hoot;
Teach me to judge its headlong pace
And dodge it with a nimble grace.

When drivers' looks and words are black,
Restrain me Lord from answering back,
O bless me with a nature meek
To bear with smiles each narrow squeak.

And if one day Thy watchful eye
Should be withdrawn and I should die
One boon I crave upon my knees:
Exonerate the driver, please.

AML

AS THE WHEELS OF LIFE TURN

YOU would have made a good wheel dog,' I said to Tovey, the black dog with the Queen Anne legs who shares my life.

I had just returned from a ten-day English idyll and had seen my first wheel dog.

Tovey looked up from a deep sleep at the mention of the word dog and then closed his eyes again, realising that we were not in danger from any canine visitors. In fact, during my absence, two of our canine friends have gone to the land where bones grow on trees. Up-the-road George and next cottage-down-the-valley Beaver were Tovey's contemporaries and we will miss them.

It was in Bath in the kitchen of a beautifully restored 18th century house in one of the lovely crescents that I learned about wheel dogs. A wheel was placed over the open fire and inside the wheel was a life-size wooden dog, the real version of which provided the motive power for turning a spit. Apparently, wheel dogs, were hired for the purpose, and a kind-hearted cook had a good supply of dogs so that a ten-minute stint inside the wheel was all that was necessary. It must have been a tiring occupation and I resisted making any remark about 'hot dogs' while the guide was explaining the historical background of the wheel dogs in that elegant town house.

I was surprised and delighted to see how the Bath civic authority has tackled these post-war years. There has been some very careful restoration and cleaning of the important squares and crescents, and the Pump Room and the Assembly Room still seemed to exude the grandeur of past times. I lived in Bath not long after the war when the bomb scars were still apparent and it was remarkable to see the work that the civic planners had done. Old buildings, if they have merit, need to be protected from the demands of those who see no beauty in age.

There is much discussion at the moment about the need to allow those who are old and who feel they have the right to die to he helped by making euthanasia legal.

Thinking of Tovey's two canine friends, perhaps some would argue that we are kinder to our pets than to people when they are incurably ill.

24

I like the gentle line in Tennyson's 'In Memoriam':

God's finger touched him, and he slept.

TWO-LETTER WORD THAT'S HARD TO SAY

I AM not one of those people who write to Agony Aunts, go to citizens' advice bureaux or even telephone Victim Support to ask for help in getting junk mail stopped. I like junk mail, although I have to own it makes going through the daily delivery of post a longish task.

Some of my favourite items are unasked-for catalogues which anxious stores and mail-order firms send me regularly. Perhaps they know that sitting in my cottage – the address of which they know down to the last detail, including my surname, Christian name and marital status – is someone who can be persuaded to buy an item the need of which had never crossed her mind until she saw it illustrated in their catalogue!

I have run a home for over fifty years without ever dreaming of possessing some of the gadgets which are on offer. I like the idea of stationing a plastic cat in the garden which lets out an impressive meow when an intruder threatens to enter the garden. On the other hand, to be greeted myself on returning home late at night by such a sound might well give me a fatal heart attack.

There were some dust-attractive doormats on offer recently, which reminded me of the St Helier store which was advertising these mats to potential customers. I telephoned the store to ask innocently what the radius was of their attraction. 'Would they,' I asked 'attract neighbours' dust from nearby houses?' The assistant at the end of the telephone told me that the only person who could answer that question was the manager, who was out of the Island. That girl will go far!

I have been tempted by the suggestion that for the outlay of a small amount of money on certain household goods I could become eligible for their next draw, in which I might well win half a million pounds or more. It was a fatal move to say I was willing, for, thereafter, I was bombarded with circulars telling me I was already the lucky winner of some enormous prize. There was a sense of urgency about these letters. I had to reply by return of post for already my name was among the lucky winners.

We are all beset by temptation in this world. The young are tempted to try drugs by being told that it is the smart thing to do. Many people get in debt by buying things which they cannot afford by the so easy access of the little plastic cards to happiness.

Saying no is difficult, but to keep out of trouble it is necessary to learn that simple word. With God's help, we can survive even the wiles of the materialistic Devil.

Most of us have Will Power; what is more difficult is having Won't Power.

TALKING THE SAME LANGUAGE

'COULD I say keep your Barnet on?' I asked friend Denise with whom I was discussing rhyming Cockney slang. She confirmed that any person born within the sound of the Bow Bells (those rung at the church of St Mary-Le-Bow) would know instantly what it meant for Barnet Fair is one of the well-known rhymes for hair.

She then taught me several other examples of rhyming slang such as apples and pears for stairs. 'Get up them apples' would not be instantly understood as a command except by those who speak the language. A gentler suggestion, 'how about a cup of Rosy', meant that a cup of tea was being offered, for every Cockney knew that Rosy Lea and tea were synonymous. I've always known that trouble and strife stood for wife which must have originally been coined to describe a somewhat bellicose partner. 'Mind me plates' is said when someone is about to stand on your feet, for plates of meat is rhyming slang for feet and only the term plates is used to describe feet. A judge is known as Barnaby Rudge and a magistrate is a garden gate. Quite a few of the rhyming Cockney slang terms did refer to the law for, no doubt, those who lived by their wits among the fraternity had a few brushes with the law before landing in the bucket and pail (jail).

Originally, rhyming Cockney slang was used so that eavesdroppers would be fooled or those in authority outwitted.

Language is a strange thing. Babies hear their first words from their mothers as they are nursed and frequently baby talk is the origin of the language of love. Later in life when couples fall in love they have their pet names for each other which are only revealed to the world when Valentine Day messages are printed in newspapers. The readers will never know who Snooky Wooky or Teddy Tail are but the loved one will know who the lover is by the secret names they call each other.

There is another language of love which is the language of silence. There are no words to express the deepest feelings. Language is not necessary. The language of silence is also used by

26

those who practise meditation when there is silent communion with God. Even without meditating, most people at the office desk, on the bus, sitting by their fireside or simply alone in a quiet place can talk to God.

> *In the silence a blackbird sang*
> *and I felt his presence in the*
> *deep quiet of the lonely wood.*

A JOURNEY TO REMEMBER

IT was the noise that brought it all back to me. Standing in what had once been the underground headquarters of the commander in chief, Western Approaches, the memories of over 50 years ago flooded back.

Known as Britain's best kept secret, Liverpool's Second World War underground HQ from where the Battle of the Atlantic was controlled from 1941-1945 has recently been opened as a museum. Tourism brochures with maps direct visitors to the place which once no one knew existed unless they had a secret pass to the HQ.

I reported there as a signals Wren in 1941 and remained for two years. I am not someone who enjoys living in the past and it was only the 50th anniversary of VE day and the attendant publicity that made me determined to make a journey of remembrance to the place where I had earned my first pay packet.

I paid the entrance fee, walked along the familiar stone corridors and entered the signals room where the noise of clattering teleprinters, typewriters and Morse code machines transported me back in time. The noise had been faithfully simulated and although the commentator stated that many signals staff suffered from appalling headaches, I could not remember that aspect of the work.

What I did remember as I stood there were the statistics on the posters which stated that 120,000 seamen had died trying to get supplies across the Atlantic in the teeth of U-boats and enemy aircraft. I remembered dancing with some of the men before they were blown up and died in a blazing oil inferno which warmed for a few moments the cold waters of the Atlantic.

As I left I thought I would buy a postcard to send the odd comrade still alive from those days. One postcard featured Churchill and another pictured the Union Jack. A third looked more hopeful, appearing to represent some battle scene. Closer scrutiny revealed it to be of the Relief of Mafeking!

I asked the girl at the desk if perhaps there were others more relevant, but they were apparently sold out.

I smiled as I walked into the sunlight. Old servicemen and women fight old battles and still the horror of today's battles sicken us as we read the war correspondents' accounts.

> *Give peace in our time*
> *0 God for we are sick*
> *of war.*

IN THE HEAT OF THE MOMENT

'I HOPE he doesn't still kiss the ground when he arrives in a country,' I said to Bennie, who was holidaying with me this month in Dubrovnik. 'If he does, there might be a slight problem with the tarmac.'

We were sitting at the time in the reception area of the hotel. Outside it was nearly 90 degrees Fahrenheit, the scale which I understand, and the newly tarmacadamed road outside was shining in the hot sun. If it were a jelly, I would say it would take some time to set.

We were having a wonderful fortnight's holiday in Croatia spending the entire time in Dubrovnik, that magical ancient walled city.

Having never been in that part of the world before and being geographically almost illiterate, despite much travel to foreign places, I was totally unprepared for the fact that the Adriatic washed the shores of the city and every morning a different cruise liner would be almost moored outside the bedroom window when I opened the curtains. Those on cruises, who came ashore on the liberty boats, must have been as thrilled as I was to wander in the narrow streets to see the ancient ramparts and to sit in the cloisters of the Franciscan monastery and visit the pharmacy where pills and potions had been dispensed since the 14th century. Our chemists' shops seem to have a rather shorter life!

The war of 1991 had done a great deal of damage to the country but Dubrovnik's old city had been beautifully restored and the townsfolk told us that this had been done with gifts from the United Nations and the Swiss Government.

Tourism is becoming the salvation of the economy and the visit of the Pope, who was due to arrive on 6 June, was a long-awaited event. The last Papal visit had been in the year 900.

We suffered only from the fact that every road had to be repaired for his arrival and it was a pity that our package holiday ended on the day before il Papa arrived so we could not see how the Popemobile fared on the sticky roads.

> *Travel not only broadens the mind,*
> *it enriches the soul and makes us aware of*
> *the beauty of God's world.*

WE ARE A MIRROR ON OUR WORLD

AT this time of the year anxious students are planning what to do if they get good enough grades to get to the university or college of their choice. The realisation has probably already dawned that not enough work has been done over the years to get the grades necessary for the courses they would like to study.

I have to admit that I find it quite difficult to get on the same wavelength of many of today's young people. They seem to talk a different language, if they speak at all. Mostly they are engrossed with a mobile phone stuck to their ear while they converse with some friend whom they probably left only minutes before. They send text messages to each other with lightning fingers. Their home life consists of a retreat to a bedroom where they play computer games of great complexity or they have playstations – about which I know nothing – and they emerge for meals only to retreat again into their private world.

Of course, the world of the playstation and the computer and mobile phone starts much earlier than the teenage years. Children of five have more understanding of the technology of today's world than I have.

I have a computer and I can use the e-mail facility to get in touch with friends or to order some item. I can surf the net, as it is called, but rarely do unless there is something which I need to know. I do not spend more time than is strictly necessary at my computer. Somewhere along the line I feel I am missing out.

The young people I know are not hoodlums or troublemakers, but they seem to be of a different breed from teenagers of yesteryear. I can talk fairly eloquently on sport and as a Manchester United supporter I can share their dismay or delight when their favourite team wins or loses. They are polite to me and if they think I am a dinosaur from another age they conceal it well.

I was sent this the other day:

> *If children live with criticism they learn to condemn. If they*
> *live with hostility they learn to fight. If they live with*

29

ridicule they learn to be shy. If they live with shame they learn to feel guilty. If they live with tolerance they learn to be patient. If they live with encouragement they learn to have confidence. If they live with praise they learn to appreciate. If they live with fairness they learn what justice is. If they live with security they learn what faith is. If they live with approval they learn to like themselves. If they live with acceptance and friendship they learn to find love and God in the world.

A SIMPLE SEARCH FOR HOPE

I HAVE always tried in this column to write in a lighthearted or gentle way of the world in which I live.

I have, nevertheless, been aware over the years of the enormous problems which some people have to face. I have listened to their stories and felt the pain of their sadness. There have been stories of loss, tales of betrayal, personal accounts of the agony of loneliness in a world where everyone else appears to have someone to love. I have done little else but listen, for there is no easily written prescription to take to the pharmacist for hearts that are broken.

It was while I was thinking of one such encounter that I found this poem. In a way, it sums up for me what life is all about. I commend it to all who are sharing another's burden or to those who feel alone at this time.

> *We told our stories*
> *That's all*
> *We sat and listened to each other*
> *And heard the journeys of each soul*
> *We sat in silence*
> *Entering each other's pain and sharing each other's*
> *joy*
> *We heard love's longing and the lonely reaching out*
> *For love and affirmation.*
> *We heard of dreams shattered. And visions fled.*
> *Of hopes and laughter turned stale and dark.*
> *We felt the pain of isolation and the bitterness of*
> *death.*
>
> *But in each brave and lonely story*
> *God's gentle life broke through.*
> *And we heard music in the darkness*

And smelled flowers in the void.

We felt the budding of creation
In the searchings of each soul
And discerned the beauty of God's hand in
Each muddy, twisted path

And God sang in each story
God's life sprang from each death,
Our sharing became one story of a simple lonely
search
For life and hope and oneness
in a world which sobs for love.
And we knew that in our sharing
God's voice with mighty breath
Was saying . . .
Love each other and take each other's hand.

   Edwina Gateley

LEARN THROUGH PLAYING THE GAME

A FRIEND found this description of golf among some old papers. She suggested that I might use it as the basis for a Saturday article. I read it through with interest and although there is an assumption in it that only men play the ancient game it does contain certain truths.

All sport, if it is played fairly and in the right spirit, should develop character and, furthermore, it ought to instill in those who play team games an unselfishness that is good training for life. Individual sports teach the discipline of practising and training for many hours, often quite alone, and this, in itself, is character forming.

I have always admired those who are amateur athletes who spend all their spare time trying to achieve better performances. They run, jump, throw and pit themselves against their own or someone else's record. Swimmers, too, deserve more recognition than they get, for their training is often very arduous and demanding and needs considerable commitment on the part of the participants and their coaches. Those whose hobby is riding know well the training needed for racing and eventing, and like all lovers of sport they have to give a great deal of themselves to their pastime.

Self-discipline is part of the Christian way of life as well as the pattern for the sport lovers, and those who are self-indulgent seldom achieve success or happiness. The golf passage below applies to life as well as to many sporting activities.

> *Golf is a science, the study of a lifetime, in which you may exhaust yourself but never your subject. It is a contest, a duel, or a melée, calling for courage, skill, strategy and self-control. It is a test of temper, a trial of honour, a revealer of character. It affords a chance to play the man and act the gentleman. It means going into God's out-of-doors, getting close to nature, fresh air, exercise, a sweeping away of mental cobwebs, genuine recreation of tired tissues. It is a cure for care, an antidote to worry. It includes companionship with friends, social intercourse, opportunities for courtesy, kindliness and generosity to an opponent, it promotes not only physical health but moral force.*

David R Forgan

LOVE ME, LOVE MY DOG

'EXCUSE ME,' the youngish woman said. 'I hope you don't mind me speaking to you but I've always wanted to meet you.'

I stopped in my tracks, flattered into stillness. After all, admirers are not thick on the ground and I was anxious to find out why she had this wish to make my acquaintance.

'Well, it's not actually you so much as Tovey I'd like to meet,' she said by way of explanation. 'I've read his book, and I read your column every week hoping you'll mention him.'

My ego trip had been short-lived. The object of her admiration was not me but the black dog with the Queen Anne legs who shares my cottage and my life.

I stopped for a little while, chatting to Tovey's admirer, and assured her that he was well, although getting more like Denis Healey. It is his eyebrows which are now rather bushy and white and they give him the air of an elder statesman.

His habits are not improving with age. Last month I thought I could trust him for a short leadless walk in the field below the cottage. I was wrong. Once a bolter, always a bolter, and he returned nearly three hours later having chased every rabbit in sight and looking sorry for himself because he had a very slightly torn ear. No doubt a blackberry bush or a piece of barbed wire had proved a temporary impediment.

It is said that leopards do not change their spots. I have never believed that they had any desire to do anything so foolish.

32

Leopards' spots become them very well. However, the saying is a reference to sinners who do not seem capable of reformation.

I have not met very many hardened sinners, but I have encountered people like Tovey who are implacably opposed to changing their behaviour even if that behaviour often lands them in trouble.

> *Teach me, God, that I am not always right, even if admitting I am wrong is difficult for me.*

HELPING US TO STEER THE RIGHT PATH

ONE reads a good deal nowadays about planned births. It seems to me that in another decade, unless something is done about it anyone will be able to produce a child at the drop of a hat.

In the light of that I do wish the swallows would read some of the research into planned births and see if the eggs could be more quickly hatched. I love to see mother and father swallow flying in and out of the garage, but my car as been standing in the open now for a very long time.

The nest which was used two years ago was deserted last year. However, this year they have returned to base. I climbed on to a step ladder to have a look and it is elegantly lined with feathers. The nest sits on a small shelf which was specially constructed for the swallow parents of two years ago and which provides a very secure foundation. They have been enormously busy flying in and out and resting on the electricity wires in between their sorties. In the recent hot weather they must have been as exhausted as the Tour de France cyclists, for they seemed to be round and round and in and out all day.

As I have mentioned the Tour de France competitors I have to own that my admiration for them is boundless. While I know that their machines have a vast selection of gears and are streamlined for speed and are as light as the manufacturers can design them, I still find the endurance of the men who ride them quite remarkable.

Of course I have been a cyclist off and on all my life. However, my cycling has never been an endurance test, but rather a matter of pedalling the shortest way from one point to an other. The notion of cycling over mountainous roads in France and then venturing through the Channel Tunnel before tackling great stretches of English roads makes me quite tired just to contemplate it. The reward of wearing the yellow jersey of the race leader must be a matter of great pride.

While on the subject of wheels and winning, I saw this quotation on a pulpit noticeboard last month. It contains a great truth.

Christianity, the steering wheel of life – not the spare wheel.

SEEING THE LIGHT

'I AM astonished that you have lasted as long as you have,' I said as I took the slender piece of glass in my hand. It was not an 18th century goblet with cutting and engraving in high or low relief. As we all know, if we have the Pictorial Encyclopedia of Antiques, such a glass or goblet can be ascribed to Thuringia and can be placed in the second quarter of the 18th century. Nor was the piece of glass in my hand an Electors' Bumper, showing the Emperor Rudolph II with seven electors. This valuable piece is from Northern Bohemia and the date of it manufacture is 1593.

Neither of these priceless goblets is in my possession but they are shown in all their glory in the photographic pages of the encyclopedia.

By now I should have whetted my readers' appetites about the priceless piece of glass I had in my possession last week. I have to own I no longer have it and when the glass collection takes place this month it will go out with the bottles and jars which have accumulated in the glass dustbin. The piece was broken but I can date it accurately to 1966 when it was placed in the fitted wardrobe in my bedroom where it has functioned most successfully as a strip light ever since!

Just occasionally, I am surprised if some piece of modern production actually functions successfully and lasts for a reasonable length of time. The little 11-inch strip light was one such piece. The wardrobe door is opened several times a day and the light comes on. As far as I know it goes out when I shut the door.

As it is my custom to end these articles with some sort of quotation it is fairly obvious that I could use the door switch theory as an example of faith. If I did not believe the light went out I would remove the new strip light and not risk wasting electricity. However, I do believe it and the longevity of the last strip light confirms my belief.

I too have loved and lost;
but without faith there would
be no light in all the world.

Helen Keller

WHEN WE NEGLECT OUR DUTIES

THE hinge on the door of the summer house broke just before we put the garden furniture away for the winter.

I hate putting away the garden furniture because it means that summer is finally over. I delay it for as long as I can, but when the leaves are falling on the table and chairs and the overall effect is somewhat sad and autumnal I know that I have to steel myself and start the winter storage operation.

The hinge broke because of my carelessness. I never allow the door to swing in the wind. I have a strut with a hook which fastens the door and I always remember to do it. What prompted me to forget on a windy day and let the door swing I do not know. However, when I came to my senses I found the screws had been torn out of the wood by the force of the wind pressure. Furthermore, I had noted during the summer that the wood was a little rotten and needed repairing, but I had ignored it. I now had a major repair job on my hands.

For readers who believe that I sit all day at a word processor writing and can do little else, I would venture to suggest that I am not altogether without other talents. I can effect minor repairs and have been known to change a ballcock in a faulty cistern which, if I remember, was no mean task. So the hinge provided me with a very minor challenge. I had, in the garage, a tube of plastic wood. I filled up the holes and the surrounding area and when it hardened I looked around for the screws and after quite a search found them. The screws, like the hinge, play a vital part in allowing the door to open and shut.

As I knelt on the granite step tightening up the screws I suddenly remembered one of the maxims which was prefixed to Old Richard's Almanac, which was written in 1758. It highlights a very important truth. Had I not neglected to shut the summerhouse door the whole operation would never have had to be undertaken and had I repaired the rotten wood before the gale all would have been well. So often it is the neglect of our duties both spiritual or physical which cause us trouble. Sometimes we put off a duty from sheer idleness or we fail to notice a job which should be done and the result is often something we live to regret.

> *A little neglect may breed mischief . . . for want of a nail, the shoe was lost; for want of a shoe, the horse was lost; and for want of a horse the rider was lost.*

WISE WORDS ON MY PILLOW

THE three little notelets have been lying in my top desk drawer ever since I returned from a holiday at a rather upmarket hotel where I was enjoying a four-day stay at reduced prices because of some wonderful offer which the management had advertised. Each night on the pillow, instead of the customary chocolate which such hotels occasionally provide as a thoughtful little gift, was a notelet. There was a different message for each night of my stay, and I brought them back with me, thinking to share them with Saturday Special.

Each was printed with the logo and name of the hotel, and underneath were written the words 'Good night. . .' Inside was a suitable verse. The one which I pulled out from the drawer contained these words:

> *Night comes like an old friend,*
> *Comforting and tranquil,*
> *As the day's activities are hushed*
> *And fade into memories.*
> *A gentle sleep is welcome,*
> *Renewing us to celebrate*
> *The glorious dawning*
> *Of a new day.*

A great deal of emphasis nowadays is placed on establishments giving good service to their customers. There are courtesy awards in Jersey as well as in other places for staff and management who endeavour to give customers the sort of attention which they deserve.

Even as I write this, I am aware that some customers, whether they are hotel guests or shoppers, behave so badly that it must be a struggle for a member of staff to serve such people. The old adage that the customer is always right is a bitter pill to swallow when faced with someone whose ill-manners deserve to he ignored when he or she asks for service.

I can remember since I have lived in this neck of the woods when one extremely difficult customer was banned from our corner shop. The owner felt that his staff should not have to put up with the aggressive behaviour which was meted out by that particular customer.

Part of the Christian ethic is service. The example of Christ washing the feet of the disciples demonstrated this.

> *There is no greater privilege than to serve God and one's fellow human beings.*

THE WILLPOWER TO SAY NO

I HOPE telly-shopping never becomes a reality in this neck of the woods. I discovered it when holidaying in Burgundy in June. In the small auberge where we stayed there was a television in the bedroom. I inadvertently switched it on one morning at about 8.30 and found myself being offered all sorts of expensive goodies without which I was assured my life was incomplete.

The sales people were mostly a middle-aged couple who positively oozed respectability and charm. Looking at them I felt comforted by their presence in the bedroom and when they suggested that what I most needed on one morning was a Jacuzzi bath and an ironing board of such diversity I felt quite deprived because I did not have either item.

The ironing board, for the record, had all sorts of protrusions on which one could hang one's newly ironed shirts, skirts, dresses and I think might even have had a space for a cafétière so that one could make coffee in the middle of one's pressing activities. I was bedazzled by it and only just refrained from ringing up the telephone number of the supplier in Paris by becoming involved in the glories of the Jacuzzi, which seemed to be a bargain which would be hard to resist. The comforting tones of Mr and Mrs Average sitting in the studio either trying out the goods or watching glamorous people demonstrating the advantages of the various merchandise was positively soporific.

On one occasion I fell asleep and nearly missed le petit déjeuner for there was on offer a bed of such refinements that I could imagine myself sinking into the mattress and pressing a spring which would raise me up at will. That bed, they assured me, was ridiculously priced at a give-away figure.

Fortunately, I am not too adept at translating francs into sterling while at the same time getting out my credit card with which the goods could be bought, or I might have landed back at the ferry with a luxury bed, a Jacuzzi bath and a mind-boggling ironing board on the roof of the car.

As I thought of the temptation which such programmes as tele-shopping present to the more weak-minded I recalled the old saying that has appeared more than once in my columns:

> Most people have plenty of willpower; it is won't power they lack.

WHEN NATURE IS PERVERSE

THE magnolia down the valley was particularly, beautiful last month. Alas, the time has gone when I could alert friends through this column about its glory, for having caused traffic jams in the valley for several years I was distinctly unpopular with my neighbours when I suggested a trip to see the tree.

I was relieved when a fellow columnist did report this year's glorious show and was glad that I went down the valley on a day when, by some miracle, it was not raining, so I could pay my annual pilgrimage to Madame Magnolia in all her finery. The huge pink blooms were spectacular against the blue sky and I drank in the peace and the glory of it before proceeding down to Rozel Bay to speak to the ducks.

On the way back I met several of my farming friends who were still agonising about 'the planting' and my remark that perhaps rice would grow well in their paddy fields was not too well received.

Nature is sometimes very perverse. Of course, on the whole in the Island we do not have the great swings of temperature which can affect the rest of the world. True, we have fog and gales but generally speaking our climate is temperate and our soil good-natured.

This year the constant rain was depressing for those trying to get their early Jersey Royals into the ground and it also blighted the lives of those who indulge in outdoor sports. The golfers, who normally can endure rain when protected by their waterproofs, lurked despondently in the clubhouses and those who enjoy riding horses down by the cottage looked far from happy with rain pouring down their necks.

It was not just farmers and sportsmen who were frustrated by the rain, for those engaged in the building trade found outdoor work well-nigh impossible. Loss of work can mean loss of wages for builders, and waiting for the rain to stop so that foundations can be laid and outside walls constructed, was difficult this winter.

As I thought of the wet days of this winter and I remembered the beauty of the magnolia, I wondered if it had been because of the rain reaching down to the roots that the tree had responded so well.

> *Just as the rain refreshes the thirsty land*
> *So shall prayer refresh my parched soul.*

THE NIGHT OF THE NEEDLE

'I AM not enjoying lying on the floor sewing this flounce on,' I said to Tovey, the black dog who shares my life.

Tovey was lying beside me looking, admiringly at my ability to sew while lying flat on my stomach.

Lest there are those who think that I have now entered the haute couture field I ought to clarify things. The matter of the loose covers came to a head last month and I finally decided to make the change. I ordered the kind which are ready-made and with great care chose the design of the chairs which I thought deserved a new outfit for the New Year.

All was well until I discovered that the flounces came separately and needed to be sewn on. And it was sewing the flounces on the chairs which nearly proved my undoing.

I am not the greatest seamstress in the world. In fact, I would go further and say that I am one of the poorest needlewomen I know. It began when I had to stitch my shoe bag at the age of five with my initials as a form of decoration in the middle of the bag. I was the only child in a class of 30 who actually had a shoe bag divided in two because I had gone through the two sides.

My confidence in myself as a needlewoman has never been restored - and as I lay on the floor stitching the flounces on, I broke one needle, lost my thimble, and finally pierced my thumb.

Tovey kept thrusting his ball under my nose, so the whole operation was fraught with difficulties.

The new loose covers look well. They do not 'go' too well with the carpet, but then my sitting room carpet does not lend itself to covers which rival its exotic pattern.

On the night of the flounce-sewing operation I remembered when I went to bed that the very first home ciné film show which my brother and I had presented a memorable Harold Lloyd epic comedy which ended with a Longfellow quotation. As I fell into an exhausted sleep the words came back to me:

> Something attempted, something done has earned a night's repose.

A BIRD IN THE HAND

'IT'S a surprise,' our friend Gyn said when we were driving towards Guerande, that delightful old walled city in the Loire Atlantique district of France.

There is nothing I like more than surprises when on holiday – always provided they are genuine delights and not nasty shocks which one sometimes encounters when far from home.

On this occasion Bennie, my long-suffering holiday companion, and I were promised a surprise at half past five o'clock in the afternoon in Guerande. We know the area well because we are lent a house every year by two good and generous friends whose names I shall not mention in case they get besieged by others hoping to muscle in on our good fortune.

Last year we were enlivened by a visit to the Planet Sauvage near Nantes, where an encounter with an ostrich proved a little too exciting for us. Ostriches are all right in their place, but quite frankly their place is not in the car. We were obeying the rules, as one does in safari parks the world over, and not getting out of the car but had the windows wide open in order to throw the animals goodies which we purchased at the entrance. This particular ostrich had a positive obsession with peanuts and, not content with the one or two nuts generously thrown out of the window, he put his head into the car and started abstracting nuts from the lap of one of the passengers who happened to be quite phobic about all creatures with wings.

Steering the car with an ostrich attached is not easy, and with one passenger all but fainting and two so convulsed with mirth as to be quite helpless, Paul the driver performed a feat of steering worthy of Michael Schumacher in a chicane.

This year we had no Planet Sauvage as our surprise, but had instead a concert by the Porcawl Cawl Male Voice Choir in the lovely old church in the town. Two out of the four of us were Welsh, and as the familiar songs were sung in the way only a Welsh male voice choir can render them, it was certainly an unexpected delight.

I had hoped that they would sing my favourite Cwm Rhondda setting of one of the well-known hymns, but that was not on the programme so I hummed it softly as we journeyed home.

> *Guide me 0 thou great Jehovah,*
> *Pilgrim through this barren land,*
> *I am weak but thou art mighty,*
> *Guide me with thy powerful hand.*

A MESSAGE THAT'S ONLY SKINDEEP

I AM not familiar with the art of tattooing. I always thought that it would be an extremely painful process involving piercing the skin with coloured dyes and making patterns which the tattooer was capable of reproducing.

I have, indeed, in naval ports where I was stationed, seen small tattooers' premises (or did they call them parlours?) which were very modest establishments with fly-blown advertisements in the windows showing the sort of designs which were related to the sea because young sailors liked to adorn themselves with anchors, crown and flags to show that they were old salts. There were those who, in the first enthusiasm of young love, had their girlfriends' names tattooed on their arms inside a heart pierced by Cupid's arrow. Old salts should have warned them that this was a dangerous step because the day might come when passion cooled and another girlfriend would object to having to read daily her predecessor's name on Jolly Jack's chest.

I was lying in bed listening to a woman being interviewed on the radio when I suddenly remembered the confessions of worried sailors telling me of their Cupid's heart tattoo problems. The interviewee had very little space apparently left on her body for any more tattooed designs. There were dragons and all sort of animals, birds and flowers climbing all over her body arms and legs. Her worry was that she was running out of space and that she was going to be denied the pleasure of feeling the tattooer's needles. She actually admitted to enjoying the sensation!

I had never heard before of anyone enjoying the actual infliction of this pain, which I was always assured by my naval friends was quite awful.

Since primeval times, men and often women have painted their bodies, and early wall paintings have shown some of these early forms of primitive art. Nowadays, as well as tattooing their bodies, some young people adorn themselves with flesh-piercing ornaments which hang from their eyebrows, lips and even tongues as some sort of statement.

Carrying banners and shouting slogans are all forms of protest or statements of belief.

> *You do not need to have 'I Love Jesus'*
> *on a car sticker.*
> *You just need to stick to Him and your*
> *life will be your witness.*

KEEP THIS UNDER YOUR HAT BUT . . .

I HAVE a desk calendar entitled 'Forgotten English' which each day provides me with a phrase or word no longer in common use. It also informs me of interesting birthdays, and I noted on Tuesday 14 October that it was the birthday of William Penn, the Quaker, reformist and colonist. The word no longer in common use was 'hat-worship'.

Apparently, William Penn did not believe in hat honour or hat homage and refused to remove his hat even in the presence of the Sovereign. In 1681, during a ceremony in which Penn was granted a colonial charter by King Charles II, Penn kept on his headgear. Noting this, King Charles removed his hat.

Penn looked at the king and said: 'Friend Charles, why dost thou not keep on thy hat?' To which the Sovereign replied: 'It is the custom of this place for only one person to remain covered at a time.'

Game, set and match, I feel, to the King.

Hat worship took on a whole meaning for me when I was asked by a dear friend if I could take to France in my car a hat for her granddaughter. It did not seem at the time to be a large request, for the girl was going to drive for three hours up from Bordeaux to fetch it. I have to own that when I put the hat box in my car I was glad I was not too heavily laden for my nine-day break in Loire Atlantique.

The hat box measured three feet across and was octagonal. Inside was a black wedding hat of the latest fashion which was to be the piece de résistance at three forthcoming weddings in France. It could be useful for Ascot or the French equivalent – a day's racing at Longchamps – perhaps.

Fashions change among the well-dressed and the young-smart in our society. I read the other day that when well-heeled women friends in London decide to have lunch together, they call each other on their mobiles and say: 'Let's do forks.' I pass on this gem of information for any of my smart young hatted readers who may not have heard of the latest term used by ladies-who-lunch.

Reverting to Penn's refusal to remove his hat as a mark of respect, I pass this on:

> Love and respect have to be earned.
> They cannot be bought or borrowed.

ACROSS THE SEA, A KINDLY LIGHT

IT was when I took Tovey out into the garden late on Monday evening that I realised it had stopped raining. I had thought, at one point on Monday, that I would never be dry again. I kept getting soaking wet and retreated into the sanctuary of my cottage, thankful that I had a dry roof over my head. Although it was not cold, I lit the fire and threw on some dry logs and mentally drew up the drawbridge. I had not been aware that during the course of the evening the rain had stopped and it had turned into a dry bright moonlight night.

When I and the black dog with the Queen Anne legs ventured forth into the garden, I looked up to the stars and the moon and uttered a little prayer of thankfulness. Tovey went off in search of rabbits in the shrubbery and I went into the side garden to see if I could see the Carteret light.

On a clear night the lighthouse on the French coast sends out its warning message to passing ships, and I like to remember the few days when I stayed in a holiday house nearby and managed to read by the light of that great beam. Admittedly there were pauses when the light was turned away from the little cluster of houses, but it was perfectly possible to read a book at night in that cottage with the uncurtained bedroom window.

From my Rozel cottage I can only see the blinking light in the far distance, but it is the same source of power which was once my gigantic bedside reading lamp. There must be, thought as I stood there, drinking in the night air, some sort of lesson to be learned from the fact that I could still see the beam although it had been reduced by distance to a mere intermittent flash. If I moved even further away I would lose sight even of that distant flash, but the lighthouse would still send forth its beam even if could not see it.

We may not see our heavenly Father but we are never out of reach of His love.

I VOW TO THEE MY CHILDREN

IT is said – and I believe it is true – that we frequently fall into traps which we vowed we would never enter. For example, how many of us have viewed the behaviour of our parents and promised that we would never treat children as we were treated? This does not mean necessarily that we had bad parenting but rather that some of the faults which they displayed we swore we would never have.

'Because I say so' was one of my father's favourite expressions when there was a clash of wills between us. I promised myself that if ever I became a parent I would explain the reason for a decision to a child and would never resort to the 'because I say so' solution. In practice it did not work out. I failed many times and fell back on that phrase when faced with an argumentative small boy when I was just too busy to indulge in long explanations.

In the workplace, too, there are pressures which affect relationships. I have heard nurses swear that when they qualify they will be kinder to their trainee nurses than were the sisters who had put them through the mill. I gather that these promises are not always kept.

In the same way, there are those in business who swear that when they get into a managerial position they will never treat their subordinates as they were treated. I imagine that these promises too are frequently forgotten, for the traps which are set for us to fall into are sometimes well concealed.

I can remember being taught by one teacher who resorted to sarcasm and irony towards those in her care. Some pupils were reduced to tears at times. It was unforgivable, and I vowed that I would never abuse anyone in the way that I and my classmates were abused by her.

Later in life I was in the WRNS and had the task of teaching others. I had to remind myself frequently that I must not resort to such methods, but occasionally I fell into the trap when the pressure was on. Pressure conceals the trap very effectively and enables us to fall in head first.

> *God, I know I am intolerant, difficult and self-opinionated at times. Help me to remember that those for whom I am responsible have the right to be given my time and my understanding, even when the pressure in on. Amen.*

ACCEPTING THE NOT SO NICE THINGS IN LIFE

'IT'S no good,' I said to Tovey, the black dog with the Queen Anne legs who shares my life, 'you are going to have a bath.'

Tovey did a quick about turn and raced at high speed from the bathroom. However, Dulcie, our depend-upon was outside the door and put an end to his escape plan. She lifted him into the bath and his ablutions began.

From being a dignified and cheerful dog he changed to a downcast, dejected and totally dependent canine who rolled his eyes as the shampoo was rubbed into his black fur.

He no longer attempts to escape from the bath for, in truth, he cannot easily jump out now that age has set certain limitations upon him. So he stood shivering and shaking and no flattery about how wonderful he would look afterwards had any effect.

Eventually, the deed was done and he finished drying himself by rubbing against the box pleats of the loose covers on the sitting room chairs! I finished off the process with my hairdryer which is, for Tovey, an infernal machine which he loathes heartily. Holding him with one hand and the dryer with the other is quite a feat and when half dry he escaped from my clutches I left him to return to the box pleats.

Our friend, dear David, told me the other day that this has been a wonderful year for fleas. As he has a special interest in selling products which fleas do not enjoy when they encounter them, he knows what he is talking about. Centrally heated houses and a long, hot summer have delighted the fleas and caused pet owners to look anxiously at their dogs and cats watching for the slightest signs of scratching.

It was the talk of fleas over the bridge table which made me decide to bath Tovey with his flea shampoo lest he was playing host to a friendly alien from Outer Space.

Not only has there been a plague of fleas in the Island, but I was driven indoors on several days this summer by an invasion of wasps. They seem to have made their headquarter up by the Butade, which is my fancy name for the summer house area, and their behaviour during several breakfasts when they wished to share the marmalade jar with me was positively threatening.

While accepting that fleas and wasps have place in God's creation, I have to own I find their presence unattractive.

> *God who made such lovely things,*
> *Why did you make the wasp who stings?*
> *And what benefit on earth are fleas*
> *Who by their presence so displease?*

A MODEL OF ENDURANCE

THERE was a very amusing article in my national newspaper the other week by Libby Purves entitled 'In Praise of the Unknown Commuter'. She suggested that as there is to be a new age dawning with super trains and electric buses and all sorts of inspired architecture – thanks to the Prince of Wales – some thought should be given to new statues. Her suggestion was a simple one. She envisaged statues strategically placed to the Unknown Commuter. I loved her suggested design of a briefcase-carrying man or woman standing with one arm upflung, shading his or her eyes as if searching for an invisible bus.

In the writer's eyes commuters are without a doubt the heroes and heroines of our age. I have to own that, when I travel in the London rush-hour, I can scarcely believe that people put up with the enormous discomfort day after day in order to get to and from their place of work. It is a shattering experience travelling by bus or tube in any crowded city when one lives in the comparative peace of our small Island. Of course we have queues. We fret and fume at traffic lights when our mini-rush hours are causing us some discomfort. However, the awfulness of overcrowded public transport systems do not really affect the majority of us greatly. Strap-hanging for a two-hour journey is not something which we daily endure.

Like Libby Purves, I think that a statue to an Unknown Commuter would be very appropriate, for commuters suffer enormous discomfort, disappointment when trains are cancelled, fear when stations are the subject of terrorist attacks and the indifference, at times, of those whose job it is to convey people with courtesy and consideration.

Thinking of statues to Unknown Commuters, I wonder who else might deserve a statue. What about a statue to the Unknown Shop Assistant who deals cheerfully and helpfully with customers, some of whom are impossibly demanding? How about a statue to the Unknown Teacher who works long and extra hours trying to help pupils who desperately need the individual attention which the timetable did not allow for in a busy day? Or what about a statue to the Unknown Refuse Collector who never grumbles at the long day but consistently and cheerfully does his unpleasant job so efficiently.

I know people who I could recommend as models for these statues and they are all examples of the Craftsman's Prayer which commuters going backwards and forwards to work also echo:

> *Give with each morning new,*
> *A job to do,*
> *And at the setting of the sun,*
> *The knowledge of a job well done.*

TRAVELLING AFAR ON A WING AND A PRAYER

I HAVE often said that more prayers are uttered as a plane takes off and lands than at any other time. People who never darken the doors of a church and have only a very faint belief in God tell me that they usually mutter a simple prayer like 'Oh God get the plane safely off the ground' at the start of a flight and usually, when the plane begins its descent, they murmur a similar prayer such as 'Oh God let it land safely'.

Passengers having only a rudimentary idea of how a plane gets off the ground in the first place put their trust in God and in the pilot.

I am constantly amazed by the fact that a machine weighing goodness knows how much when fully laden is capable of what is called 'lift-off' in rocket language. Coming down seems easier to me in my ignorance. After all, it is quite unnatural for it to be up there in the first place.

Having now shown my appalling ignorance of the principles of aerodynamics, I do not want to be educated by those who either pilot planes or know the engineering principles. I am content in my ignorance because I believe that those who fly me know exactly what they are doing. They, in turn, have to believe that the plane's designers and those who service them are competent in their fields.

There are other factors which cause plane accidents. Terrorists, whose twisted minds can devise bombs which make a plane crash, are a new factor in modern society. Hijacking seems to have given way to this new horror. All the security checks that airlines can devise can, it seems, can be circumvented by men with evil intent.

At the end of the day, for those who put their lives in the hands of others, there has got to be trust.

The prayer I say most often at the beginning of a day is one attributed to John Henry Newman. It is worth learning as a take-off and landing petition.

> *0 lord support us all the day long, until the shadows lengthen and the evening comes, and the busy world is hushed, and the fever of life is over and our work is done; then Lord, in thy mercy grant us safe lodging, and a holy rest, and peace at the last.*

SHARE AND SHARE ALIKE

UNSELFISHNESS is not generally speaking a characteristic of the dog Tovey, with the Queen Anne legs, who shares my life.

I do not make that statement idly. We have lived together for over 11 years and I have not detected in him a tendency to share with others that which he has been given or purloined for himself. Perhaps there are altruistic members of the canine fraternity who show a selflessness which is altogether admirable but my particular furry friend has no such trait.

I had forgotten this weakness in Tovey's makeup until I was forced to separate him from Topper during a walk along St Catherine's Breakwater. Topper is a much larger dog but with, I am sure, a more beautiful nature than my friend and companion.

The dogs had not met before their walk but I transported them both in my car with Dulcie, who is having Topper for a protracted holiday.

The walk began well. We reached the end of the breakwater on the upper level because Tovey is apt to steal the fish bait if I take him along the jetty where the fishermen sit rods at the ready, waiting for a nibble at their lines. Tovey's quick forays in time past removing the bait has naturally incensed those immersed in their sport.

All was going well, and in an effort to reward the dogs for their good behaviour I produced two biscuits from my pocket. Tovey naturally had the first one and he then proceeded to take Topper's biscuit from him as I proffered it. Topper naturally took offence and in no time there was the sort of fight which I think dogs probably enjoy and owners dread.

It took us a little while to separate them and I was deeply ashamed of Tovey and he got no sympathy for his bleeding ear which Topper had grasped en passant.

As I wiped the ear with disinfectant on our return I thought that we are all naturally selfish. We have to teach our children to share their toys when they are small and it is a hard lesson to learn. Fights between small brothers and sisters are often caused by selfishness and even when we grow older we still have to remember that sharing and giving makes us better people.

A man is called selfish, not for pursuing his own good but for neglecting his neighbour's.

Whatley

DAISIES, DAISIES, GIVE ME YOUR ANSWER, DO

I HAVE always like daisies. I like daisies in other people's lawns. Their white upturned faces are reminiscent of the school prizegiving in my youth, when we had to wear white dresses and sit demure, in serried ranks, waiting for the sort of dull speech which I have myself given in my adult life on such occasions.

I can remember, as though it were yesterday, the groans which I made annually at having to don the hated white dress. Of course, over the years the style changed, but it had to be a dress which conformed to the somewhat puritanical taste of our headmistress. The year when one of the sixth form decided to come in a low-cut model remains as a highlight of prize-giving occasions in my mind. Her ascent to the platform to receive her prizes brought a swift indrawing of breath from the row of staff and a gasp of admiration from the entire school.

Strange that the daisies should have triggered off that piquant memory.

To return to the daisies themselves – which at this time of the year mount a positive assault on my top lawn. The expression 'top' is in itself an example of *folie de grandeur*. I used to have a top and a bottom lawn, but the lower area, once under tailored grass, is now a wildlife garden. It is admired by conservationists who see the violets, primroses, wild lupins and a myriad dandelions as my contribution to their cause.

But the small top piece of grass should be a tailored weed-free sward. It resembles a daisy and dandelion reservation this year. Every passing seed from a dandelion head last year found a welcome in the top lawn mat. Every daisy which found itself homeless in the present climate of housing shortage has found refuge in my garden.

I do not really want to know about selective weedkillers. I am a purist and nightly I am digging them out with the forked daisy tool. Already the top lawn looks like a refuge for a new species of giant worms, but I shall win in the end. I am putting the victims down in the wildlife area where they must make a new life for themselves.

Making a new life is not easy for a person or for a daisy. The desire to creep back to the old place, the old ways, the old habits is very strong.

> *Help me, God, to adapt to what is necessary for my wellbeing. With your help I can do anything.*

PACK UP YOUR TROUBLES

I THREW the new cassette tape across the room. It narrowly missed the rather highly polished and pleasant circular table and came to rest under the sofa.

I sat for a few moments recovering my temper before going to retrieve it. There was nothing wrong, as far as I knew, with the contents of the cassette. My anger was not directed against those who had made the recording, nor was it because of disappointment that the composer should have wasted his talents on such a work. It was not a tape I already possessed, so my anger was not because of disappointment at being given a duplicate tape. What had occasioned the fit of rage was my inability to undo the cellophane wrapper which enclosed the plastic container which held the tape. It was so securely wrapped that I had struggled for some minutes to undo the packaging and then frustration took over and I threw it across the room.

No one who knows me well would ever say that I am by nature the most patient of people. Shakespeare may well have coined the phrase 'Like Patience on a monument smiling at grief'. The Bard could never have used such a phrase to describe me.

I sit on no monuments smiling when it comes to undoing modern packaging. I believe that the manufacturers have some inbuilt problem when it comes to marketing their goods. They may promote them well, advertise them well, even sell them successfully but when it comes to wrapping them up they seem to have some Machiavellian desire to drive the recipient insane.

Before I threw the cassette across the room I had broken two nails and cut myself with the sharp pair of scissors which I use for such battles. Finally I gave a fair wind to the cassette and watched it ricochet off the table and find a final resting place.

I am sure I am not alone in finding opening plastic wrapped objects an infuriating pastime. On the other hand some people appear to have gifts for such matters which I do not possess.

Patience is certainly something we can all cultivate, and the determination to do a job – however difficult – well is also a challenge which we should not try to avoid.

My quotation for today is not scriptural or philosophical. It is, however, factual, and when I read it in a book which contained women's movement bias I found myself smiling. It concerns achievement of a very special sort.

Remember, Ginger Rogers did everything Fired Astaire did,
but she did it backwards and in high heels.

Faith Whittlesey

POURING OIL ON TROUBLED WATERS

I HAVE been thinking a good deal recently about the three Rs – not about reading, writing and arithmetic, but about recession, redundancy and rejection. These three Rs are suddenly very much a part of our contemporary society. The good old days of full employment and the expectation of a continuing rise in our standard of living are no longer certainties.

It is no good burying our heads in the sand like ostriches and pretending that recession is just a word which applies to other people. I have friends who have lost their jobs. Some have been told that they have been 'phased out' because computerisation has taken over the work they once did, and others have been told that the cutbacks in their particular field of employment have meant that they are superfluous to the company for which they worked.

For some the news has come like a bolt from the blue, and for others the growing suspicion that one day the axe would fall suddenly became a reality.

In large firms there are skilled counsellors who are able to help those whose world has suddenly tumbled around their ears. With mortgages to pay, school fees to be met and the awful realisation that suddenly there is no salary cheque or weekly pay packet, it is scarcely surprising that some people just cannot cope with the situation.

It is not just coping materially which is difficult. Recession and redundancy are the first of the three Rs, but rejection is the third, and this feeling of being no longer wanted is one of the most difficult experiences which the dismissed employee has to take on board. Self-worth is a very important part of our makeup, and when this is diminished by the loss of one's working role then very real problems can arise.

It is necessary for all of us to understand just what sort of a personal crisis those who are undergoing the three Rs are facing. The most important role families and friends can play is in adding a fourth R to the situation – that of reassurance.

Reassurance is the oil that is needed when self-respect is grinding to a halt.

AT THE GATE OF THE YEAR

I CAN remember listening to King George VI speaking to the nation in his Christmas broadcast in 1939. It was before the days of televised broadcasts of the Sovereign's Christmas greetings. It was also before the days of transistorised radios and the very notion of walking about with a radio cassette strapped to one's chest and a pair of earphones was beyond anyone's imaginings. We had just progressed from the days of having to carry wireless batteries to have them recharged.

We possessed a mahogany radiogram which was the envy of my schoolfriends. It was a handsome piece of furniture with Queen Anne legs resembling the splay feet feet of my friend Tovey, the black dog who shares my life.

We had gathered around the radiogram on that fateful Sunday in September when Neville Chamberlain told us that we were at war with Germany. Three months later, on Christmas Day 1939, we listened in silence to the King's speech. He did not have an easy time making a speech, for his stammer was very noticeable, and these were the days of live broadcasts. No editor's knife eliminated the hesitations.

We all prayed as we sat there that he would get through his speech and breathed a collective sigh of relief when it was over.

It was a memorable speech, for the nation was poised on the edge of a war, the outcome of which we did not know. We were aware of the enormous might of the German forces and of the pitifully inadequate preparations for war which our government had made. We were on the brink of an abyss, and although I was still at school I can remember the feeling of foreboding at that time.

It was a stroke of genius that the King chose to end his message with words which I have quoted before but never tire of remembering. Those words gave great comfort to me then, and they do still as a new year stretches ahead.

> *And I said to the man who stood at the gate of the year:*
> *"Give me a light that I may tread safely into the unknown."*
> *And he replied: "Go out into the darkness and put your*
> *hand into the hand of God. That shall be to you better than*
> *light and safer than a known way."*

M L Haskins

A FRIENDLY INVASION OF PRIVACY

SPACE invaders are not only those daring people who are the stars in sci-fi stories or who are to be seen on our television screens fighting wars in outer space with people from other planets who have strangely distorted faces and bodies and who seem to be possessed of not only magical powers, but peculiarly malevolent ideas as well. These characters are, it is true, inhabitants of outer space, but there are apparently other space invaders who live on our planet.

Teenagers frequently complain about having their space invaded. Their spaces, if I recall the teenage years, are sometimes bedrooms which resemble battlefields of unmade beds, bulging cupboards, gaping drawers which are full to the point of bursting and with a carpet positively strewn with clothing and shoes which are never put away.

I had a dearly-loved American niece who spent several of her teenage years here in Jersey, and whenever I ventured into her bedroom I was amazed that someone who never seemed to dress except in old jeans and long sweaters appeared to have a multitude of clothes scattered all round the quite large room which she inhabited. If she wore some of these garments it must have been in the night, for the uniform jeans and sweater had to be put in the washing machine for instant wear the next day.

Her bedroom was, however, on the whole, her refuge and I entered it only when there was some dire necessity, such as suggesting that if she did not get up she would be late for school. On such occasions I risked invading her space.

However, it is not just physical space which we invade. Sometimes we are naturally reluctant to allow people, whether they are young or old, to live their own lives.

The ghastly drug culture which abounds in Jersey is a nightmare for parents who hesitate to invade their offspring's privacy, but by ignoring the danger signals they can reap a terrible harvest of despair.

Give us wisdom, God, to know when to offer a helping hand and a listening ear to those who are too obstinate to ask for help.

YOU DIRTY RAT!

I WAS extremely relieved to note that Tovey, the dog with the Queen Anne legs, took the question of the rat in the drive very seriously.

I was sitting at my desk when I saw him. I know that the hymn 'All things bright and beautiful, all creatures great and small' must include rats in our Maker's Grand Plan, but I am incapable of living in harmony with rats.

I am now entering my 25th year of life in the cottage, and that was the first rat I had seen in the garden. My reaction was instant. 'Tovey!' I yelled in stentorian tones. 'Get him!'

Tovey is a seagull hunter and rushed out of the door with his head in the air looking for airborne prey. The rat leapt into the shrubbery and promptly disappeared. By the time I had caught Tovey and forced his nose on to the gravel where the rat had been, I imagine that the rat was miles away.

Tovey was greatly aggrieved to find himself treated in such a cavalier manner. At first he thought I had gone totally off my trolley – a position he has sometimes suspected in the past. However, he is not a terrier for nothing, and suddenly the reason for having his nose ground into the granite gravel chippings occurred to him. He started to sniff and then went off, nose to ground, hot on the trail.

I would like to think that my yelling and his sniffing frightened our friend Ratty so that he will return no more. If he does, I think Tovey may well tell him that there is no welcome on the mat for furry friends.

I was surprised that it took Tovey some little time to realise that I wanted him to pick up the trail and deal with the situation. It could be that long ago, when Tovey was a Guernsey stray, he shared the odd crust with a furry friend. Certainly when one is down on one's luck and foraging for food, I imagine that other vagrants become one's friends. Seeing the homeless occupants of cardboard city in London, I would think that there is some close cameraderie among them in their shared plight.

It is when we are fighting to survive that the encouragement of a friend is worth more than a hand-out.

SHAKE YOUR HEAD FROM SIDE TO SIDE

'THEY look as if they ought to be wearing bras,' a friend of mine said.

We were discussing the performance-enhancing drugs which are much beloved by athletes today. As my friend is herself a hammer thrower of some distinction and knows very well the international athletic scene in which she is a distinguished participator I listened to her with interest.

She pumps iron in order to train and I have to own that my ten minutes on the exercise bicycle in the bathroom pales into insignificance compared with the rigours of serious bodybuilding exercises. As my exercise cycling is not so much an attempt to build up my body but to reduce it, there are no serious grounds for comparison.

As we sat talking and I contributed all I knew about caber throwing, which I used to watch at the Highland Games in my youth, I realised that those who throw the hammer and discus are often intent upon winning at any cost. They are a very different bowl of porridge from the kilt-clad, vested participants of my youth. They are not all content with legally developing muscle strength but enter into the darker world of anabolic steroids to add to their body tissue. In time, the men develop the sort of pectoral muscles which do make one wonder if the need for some form of uplift bra might be appropriate!

As I thought about the murky world of illegal drugs in the field of sport, I hoped that those who wish to have drugs legalised will not win their fight. I am totally opposed to all forms of drug-taking unless they are prescribed by the medical profession for those who have need of them because of ill health. I cannot accept that soft drugs do not lead on to the taking of hard drugs in many cases. The tragedies which occur in families when a member becomes a drug addict are enormous.

For those readers who will chide me and say that alcohol is no less of a drug than marijuana, I have to agree. I do not happen to indulge in alcohol because I believe that one should be able to battle through the choppy currents of life without false stimulants.

While on the subject of exercise and drugs, I would remind all those who are tempted to remember this wise saying:

> The best exercise is to shake the head front side to side when offered an anything that harms the body.

RAISING A FAMILY ON LOVE

AT first I wondered if I should have got planning permission for it. I then wondered if the Housing Committee would be interested and would rate it A-J or whether it would fall into the K category of the wealthy resident's abode.

It is such a beautiful house with a pitched roof and the possibility of a loft conversion. Imaginatively designed as an open courtyard property and painted in green with white almost Moorish style openings on the ground floor, the house which Tom-Up-The-Road built is our new feature for the birds.

I have to admit that the birds behaved strangely at first. Their old feeding table had collapsed with the weight of passing seagulls stealing the food and I suggested to my neighbour and friend that I would like a covered replacement.

It is distinctly seagull-proof and after five days my friend the robin decided to risk coming in for a morning crumb of old fruit cake. Once he had shown the way, the sparrows followed and the tits were not far behind.

It has been a strange period for me, not having the birds while the building was under way and then the reluctance of my feathered friends to try out their new premises was worrying.

There is a round hole with a little step at either end giving loft access, so I am hoping that someone will think of building up there and bringing up a family.

There is much publicity about the Year of the Family and I am hoping that perhaps during these 12 months people will realise that family life is something which is valuable and worthwhile.

We all know the tensions that can build up in every relationship and these can cause many problems. From the early years, when parents are kept awake at night by crying babies, to the years when they stay up late with fear in their hearts waiting for teenagers to come home after a night out, there are anxious times. Tensions can also cause marriages to founder and other peoples' wives or husbands may seem more attractive and then lust rather than love can ruin a relationship.

Bless families everywhere and make us always aware of the needs of those who have no one to love.

WHAT'S IN A NAME?

I WAS thinking the other day, after a baptismal service, about the names we give children. Consideration about a name often begins almost as soon as a child is conceived. Nowadays it is possible to know what the sex of a child will be before it is born, so parents do not have to agonise about whether it will be William or Willhelmina until the child is delivered.

Strangely enough, several of my young married friends who have become pregnant have told me that they asked not to be told whether they were going to have a boy or a girl. 'We'd rather wait and see,' is what most of them have told me. It is not that they are not curious to know, but it is almost as if they feel it would be wrong to find out.

When the baby is born, the list of possible names is produced. There is no longer a tradition demanding that the names of grandparents should be incorporated in the latest addition to the family circle, so there is much more of a free choice than there was some fifty years ago. Fashions about names change and I have, among my newest acquaintances, a Naomi, a Joshua and a Benjamin. Perhaps there is a return to old Jewish names in this modern era.

When we are given our names, we cannot influence the choice. What is extraordinary is how, as the years go on, our name becomes associated with us, and so for our friends and acquaintances, as well as our family, that name has special significance.

When we have to fill in forms for passports, driving licences and the like we have to write our full names and when we witness someone's signature we have to ensure that it is the person to whom the document refers who is signing it in our presence.

Our names are our means of identification. I heard recently of one small boy who, after his first day at school, was asked by his mother what he had learned. He thought for a little time, then replied: 'I learned that my name isn't Precious – it's Henry.'

Occasionally, a name is spoiled for us because the person who bore the name was unkind or did us a disservice. More often, I think a name is dear to us because it is the name of a person who has been an example to us of goodness and loving kindness.

And so for all who follow the Christian way of life, the name of Jesus is of supreme importance.

At the name of Jesus every knee shall bow.

WHO CARES FOR THE CARERS?

THE question is sometimes asked now: 'Who cares for the carers?'

Such a question applies to those who have the unenviable task often of caring for aged relatives when they have become dependent and sometimes difficult in the closing years of their lives. The carers find themselves in need of support and this is too often overlooked.

There are other areas of concern when one considers those in the community who have to shoulder sometimes very heavy burdens. Certain jobs provide those who perform them with built-in strain factors. The caring professions have their share of casualties, for sometimes the demands made upon those who do very often unenviable tasks are very great.

Criticising social workers has become a fashionable ploy of late. No doubt some make mistakes, but the vast majority are coping with the casualties of our modern society with compassion and professional skill. The children's departments of most local authorities could give hair-raising accounts of those who need support and the help which dedicated workers give can cause its own enormous pressure.

I have known, over the years, a number of probation officers who seem to me to be asked to fulfil a very demanding role. They have, somehow, to form relationships with those whose behaviour has made the bonding of such relationships very difficult. They are almost too tired to enjoy the little free time they have earned.

Those who work in the caring professions are often drained physically, emotionally and spiritually. So, for any who are finding their batteries hard to charge could I commend this prayer:

> O God, my battery is flat and needs recharging – be my jump-lead and startle me into new life.

NEVER LIE TO YOUR LAWYER

'MATRIMONIAL; Separation; Maintenance; Injunctions; Wardship; Custody; Access; Legal Aid Work Undertaken. Conveyancing £180.'

That advertisement in a weekly religious paper from a firm of solicitors made me realise how life is changing. The fees for the sadnesses of broken marriages were not mentioned, but at least if one were buying a property the fee for the conveyancing by this particular firm of solicitors was clearly stated.

I had been aware that changes had taken place in UK legislation which enabled legal firms to advertise not only their services but their charges, but it was more the pathos of family breakdown which seemed to constitute a large part of that particular firm's practice.

Until recently I had been somewhat addicted to watching a soap opera about the American legal system. Called 'LA Law', the series had won me over at first because had been interested in some of the cases which the lawyers in that practice had undertaken. However, as time has gone on, I have detected that the loves and lusts of the partners in the practice seem to have become more important than the causes of their clients.

In an effort perhaps to redress the balance, one episode shown last month depicted a man sentenced to death actually in the electric chair. I found this portrayal unacceptable. It was not entertainment. It was not educational. If it were an attempt to shock the American viewer into believing that the death penalty is a barbaric means of ending someone's life, I suppose that it had some value.

This particular episode had a strong storyline. The man who went to the electric chair had asked a lawyer from the firm to try to enter a last-minute plea for mercy on the grounds that they had been boyhood friends. The lawyer accepted the brief but failed to get the panel of judges to change their collective minds. The agony of that attorney, who did not really know if his client was speaking the truth, was extremely well portrayed and really heartrending.

I wonder how many of my readers know this quotation from an unknown source.

> There are three persons you should never deceive. Your physician, your confessor and your lawyer.

THANKS FOR SPRING MEMORIES

I AM glad to greet the flowering currant bush, although it has an unfortunate perfume so reminiscent of tomcat that I am surprised that Tovey, the dog with the Queen Anne legs who shares my life, does not get over-excited. However, despite its scent, the sight of the first pink flowers on the bush always gladdens my heart. It really is a harbinger of spring in my garden and tries to beat the japonica which provides a thorny guard by the front door of the cottage.

These are swiftly followed by the white magnolia tree which has been so reluctant to grow, rather like a sickly child, but is now a respectable size and this year had a goodly show of big, white, tulip-like flowers.

Swift on the heels of the flowering currant, the magnolia and the japonica comes the Clematis montana, which has been less showy over these past few years because of my too vigorous pruning. It does not match the japonica because it is a rather pale pink but, like the other flowering shrubs and trees, it gladdens my heart in the early spring days.

Although there is a good deal of instant gardening nowadays, with pot-rooted plants and shrubs, it takes time for them to grow into respectable members of the garden family. The wistaria, for example, came as a small cutting and was put into the ground on the west wall of the garage. Mr B, who, in the early days of the garden, was my adviser and helper, stated that wistarias liked the west aspect to start their life. Certainly, that proved to be good advice for it now covers the garage wall and has come round to the south of the garage round the granary and is now vying with the clematis for the south wall of the cottage. The little thin cutting is now a thick trunk of about a foot in diameter and all that growth has taken place in just under 20 years.

I could never be the gardening correspondent of this or any other journal or magazine for I never did know the Latin names for the flowers, shrubs and trees as Mr B did. All I do know is who gave me certain plants, and some of them, like Mr B, are now gardening in the Elysian fields but their plants live on.

> Ye speak of frail humanity;
> How man shall flourish like you
> And shall fall:
> But ah! ye speak of heavenly love as well
> And say, the God of flowers is
> God of all.

From 'Flowers' by Henry Francis Lyte

STANDING THE TEST OF TIME

I SAW it by the side of the road which joins the little lane which runs down to the bay past my cottage. It had obviously been run over and looked very much the worse for wear.

Readers of a nervous disposition can safely read on, for what I saw had never been alive but was in a strange way dear to me. I must have dropped it on a walk the previous day and unfeeling motorists had run it over with their insensitive tyres. They could not have known that what lay there had shared my life for some years. I had not bought it in the first place but it had been left in the cottage by some visitor who had not returned to claim it, and as I had no idea who the owner was it became part of my wardrobe.

At one stage these were high fashion in the Fifties and Sixties. Even the Queen was seen wearing one at an informal race meeting. One would not have seen Her Majesty wearing one at Ascot, but at Badminton it would have not been a subject of raised eyebrows.

I picked up my lost treasure tenderly and carried it home. It was little the worse for wear for it had not the built-in obsolescence of present day fashion garments. It was, of course, rather dirty and I plunged it into the sink with one of the detergents which the manufacturers have assured me will restore everything to pristine cleanliness.

I am by habit a 'soaker', for long before the days of owning a washing machine I found soaking made washing easier.

Two hours later, I pulled it out and it was glistening and clean and ready for my next foray in the rain. It is, as plastic hoods go, a winner. It is decorated with little roses and although it does nothing for my appearance, it keeps my hair dry.

The high-fashion plastic hoods of the Fifties did nothing for anyone's looks, but nothing has been invented since which actually protects the coiffeur so effectively from disaster.

As I thought of my newly restored plastic protector, I thought how some things stand the test of time because nothing has been invented to improve upon them.

Mankind never loses any good thing, physical, intellectual,
or moral, till it finds a better, then the loss is a gain.'

Theodore Parker

MAINTAINING AN APPETITE FOR LIFE

I DID not know until this week that squirrels liked Danish pastry pecan pie. After all, it is not the sort of culinary delight which is usually fed to squirrels, and I doubt that any scientific research has been done on the subject. However, if any such experiments are currently being done, I could write to the authorities and describe how, on a fine November day in the year 2000 in the Vallée de Rozel, Jersey, an extremely handsome red squirrel polished off the remnants of a rather elderly Danish pastry pecan pie with huge enjoyment.

Robin, for whom this delight had been put on the bird table, had a rather long lie-in and was beaten to the feast by the red furry gentleman.

It could well be that this item of news might not be described as earth-shattering, unless of course, one were a hungry robin for whom pecan Danish pastry was a longed-for delight. On the other hand, in a world where the news is almost invariably heart-breaking it is perhaps of passing interest to note my observations about the eating habits of our red long-tailed furry friends.

It happened in the same week when Remembrance Day was being observed, and I found myself amazed as I watched on my television screen excerpts from the Cenotaph service in Whitehall. What amazed me was the fact that those marching to lay their wreaths were largely my contemporaries. The survivors of the 1914-18 war are very thin on the ground now, and even the Chelsea Pensioners in their brilliant red coats once served with me in the more recent wars.

I knew all this before I watched the parade, but every one of my peers looked old whereas I, sitting in my cottage, am as young as I was in those difficult days of war.

I ought perhaps to qualify that, because I am naturally older but do not see myself as old. I am still as young inside as I ever was, and the saying that we are as young as we feel is very appropriate.

This quotation is not particularly moralistic or theological, but it struck a chord with me. It is American, so the rhyming of grin and been is acceptable.

I awfully aware that my youth has been spent,
that my get up go has got up and went.
But I really don't mind, when I think with a grin
of all the grand places my get up has been.

THE TRUTH, THE HALF-TRUTH, AND SOMETHING BUT THE TRUTH

I WONDER how many lies we tell in an average week.

I can hear shocked indrawing of breath as my readers consider that first sentence. Yet in an average week, we do not always speak the absolute truth, and we do this by half-truths and by silence. For example, we often speak a half-truth because we are afraid that speaking the absolute truth will be hurtful.

'How do you like my new hairstyle?' is, for example, a question which men and women have to answer with care. Unisex in hairdressing does not just mean sharing the same hairdressing salon; it also means that men, in some cases, have in recent years begun to have their hair dyed, permed, blow-dried and styled in much the same way as women. A man who once had straight dark hair can emerge from the salon as a blonde with a mass of curls. Parents who had despaired in the past because of their sons' refusal to have their hair cut to what the parents considered a reasonable length are faced today with rebellion from both sons and daughters.

I do not myself prefer the modern trend whereby adolescents like to resemble some of the more exotic birds of the tropical jungle. However, I have observed over the years how styles do change, and by the time the young have left the nest they are frequently more conservative than their parents.

What has this to do with telling the truth? It was simply an example of how, faced with a startling new hairstyle or dress or interior decoration, we are sometimes hard put to it to speak the truth. Secretly we think that the hair, the dress or the décor looks appalling, but we hesitate to hurt the person who has chosen the style so we murmur tactfully something that is far from the truth.

At other times in life we stay silent when we should speak. This is because we are afraid that speaking the truth will cause trouble. We do not want to reveal how we feel about something in case we are then held up to ridicule. We may be thought to be old-fashioned or narrow-minded or even – perish the thought – one of the Jesus people! So we stay silent. It is as good as telling a lie.

It was Adrienne Rich who coined this phrase:

Lying is done with words and also with silence.

WHY I'M PLEASED I WAS GIVEN A SECOND CHANCE

AS I walked over the little road outside the cottage to a neighbour's home carrying the drum marked 'Floating Fish Food', I was glad I had been given a second chance.

Readers of this column may recall that some months ago I had been the Relief Goldfish Feeder when the Number One substitute had had to desert her post. I had not fully absorbed the instructions and, being unfamiliar with feeding a tank of goldfish, I had been somewhat over generous in the helpings. It would be boring to repeat how I watched, with mounting horror, the bloated corpses floating to the surface.

My subsequent attempts at goldfish substitution had not been a success, and I thought that I would never again be asked to assume the mantle of responsibility. However, I was called upon to step into the breach, or rather into the fish pond area, and feed the outdoor fish last week. They swim about in two ponds: the upper pond is inhabited by a superior brand of fish and, in the lower reaches, there are those of rather less significant parentage.

I was given detailed instructions – not like the last time, when I mistakenly relied on my own initiative in the feeding arrangements. At the time of writing nothing is floating on the top of the water.

When I was asked about the fish I accepted gladly because I felt I was being given a second chance, but when a gerbil was mentioned, I said quite simply: 'I don't do gerbils.'

Pondering in the Granary about the whole philosophy of the Second Chance doctrine, I thought how important it is to remember that we have to give each other not only a second but sometimes a third, fourth or even many chances. We do not always get relationships or other aspects of human behaviour right the first time. We frequently arrive at maturity by many false starts and failures, and if we do not give each other the chance to try again, we fall short of being the sort of people whom God wants us to be.

It may seem a far cry from feeding fish to unfaithfulness in relationships, but I have seen so much bitterness between partners because of the inability of the one to forgive the other and to offer a clean slate in beginning again.

> . . . *and forgive us our sins, as we too forgive everyone who fails in his duty to us.*

Luke IIIv4 (Barclay translation)

WE SHOULD ALL LEARN THE LANGUAGE OF LOVE

'THERE'S a cow down,' the member of the honorary police force said to me as he motioned to me to stop as I was driving home after a busy morning last week.

Things had not gone smoothly as I tried to do too many things in too short a time. I had made a list of shopping and visits in an effort to remind myself of what had to be achieved and, as happens so often nowadays, my expectations had exceeded my performance.

Turning the corner into the road which is only a short walk from the cottage the hold-up occurred. A small group had gathered and it did not take a Chief Inspector Morse to assess the situation. There was a yellow car with a badly damaged front wing and a cow was lying down in the road in the position which all of cows adopt when they are resting or expecting a shower of rain. I have always been told that they lie down to cover a patch of grass so that it will be dry when the rain stops. It seems a sensible thing to do. However, this cow was not on a patch of grass; it was on the road and for those of us who are country dwellers the expression the cow or the horse 'is down' has only one meaning. The animal is sick.

By the side of the road sitting on the bank was a young woman in tears. Again it would not have taken Morse or his sergeant to diagnose that this was the driver of the car. I got out of my car and went over to see if she were hurt or in need of comfort. She did not appear to be hurt so I sat down beside her and put my arm round her and uttered the conventional words of comfort. However, they fell on deaf ears. She indicated that she could not speak English.

'Polish?' I asked and she nodded. At that point I realised how awful it must be for her to he involved in this sort of incident in a strange country with people speaking a foreign language and be totally unable to communicate. Fortunately, in a few minutes a farmer appeared with a young man, who rushed to the girl and took her in his arms and spoke comfortingly in the language they had both learned as children.

The language which everyone can learn is the language of love.

A BREED APART

FOR the past 13 years, as soon as I switched on my word-processor to write this article – or indeed any other article – Tovey, the dog with the Queen Anne legs who shared my life, would leap on to his stool beside me with a rubber bone or some similar toy in his mouth. He reckoned that if I were going to play with my toy, he would do the same.

This has been a wretched week, and if there are readers of my column who are not animal lovers, they must forgive me for writing once more about him, for his death has left me very bereft.

A great emphasis nowadays is put by psychologists and psychiatrists on the need for bonding in relationships, and Tovey and I were very closely bonded. I have never been without a dog, and each one has been special to me, but Tovey was such a scallywag in his youth that I had perforce to give him more attention than had been necessary with my other dogs.

In the book we wrote together he stated: 'I wondered if, after all my wanderings, I had really met My Match. It was a sobering thought and one that was entirely strange to me.'

He had no pedigree, but if a bolter breed existed he would have won best of breed at Cruft's. He was an escapologist who made Houdini, the greatest exponent of the art, look like an amateur. I apologise to those who have got bored over the years hearing about his escapades.

I have never lived without a dog, for I have always believed that the spirit of the one goes into the next. There will, however, never be another Tovey. He was unique, and would come with me to church when I was preaching. He occupied the pulpit with unaccustomed decorum and never let me down on such occasions. He toured the Island's schools with me when we conducted morning assembly, and generations of schoolchildren knew him. We were due to go to d'Hautrée this week but somehow my heart was too heavy to go alone.

> *When the Man waked up he said, 'What is Wild Dog doing here?' And the Woman said, 'His name is not Wild Dog any more, But the First Friend, Because he will be our friend For always and always and always.*

> Rudyard Kipling

SPELLBOUND BY THE WEB OF NATURE

WATERING the garden last month with the hose which I left permanently unwound because it seemed to be in nightly use, I noticed an unusual sight. I was making a rainbow as I watered the sweet peas. I stood there playing the water on the flowers, which seemed permanently thirsty, when a small rainbow between me and the sweet peas appeared. The sky was red with the setting sun and somehow the light on the spray of water was enabling me to make my own rainbow.

I did not want to switch the water off, for I was enjoying the sight of the rainbow colours dancing a few feet away from me. It was a magical moment in the garden and I longed to prolong it. Sadly, the redness soon went out of the sky, the light changed and my rainbow was gone.

As I turned in disappointment, I swung the hose round and Barclay, who always keeps his distance at watering time, took the full blast of the water. As he shook himself, he gave me the sort of withering look that only he can give.

He is not a dog who enjoys being hosed by a careless owner and his displeasure was obvious. As I turned to comfort him, my eye fell upon a spider's web which was caught up in the honeysuckle round the Butade.

The Butade, as regular readers of this column will know, is the garden châlet which once stood at the bottom of the garden but which I had moved when the slope up from it became tedious. It now stands within easy distance and I enjoy the little stove and kettle which boils water for my breakfast cup of tea.

I put down the hose after the rainbow delight and examined the spider's web. It was most intricately woven, and although I knew it was the spider's trap to catch a passing fly, I could not but admire the intricacy of the pattern.

On the Saturday following the rainbow miracle and Barclay's unfortunate dousing, friend Bob and I were lunching up by the Butade. He was wearing a blue T-shirt with writing on it. It took me a little time to decipher the words, for it kept moving as he ate! Remembering my spider's web of a day or two I before, I thought how true the words written on his shirt were. For they were to do with the care of God's world:

> *The world is as delicate and as complicated as a spider's web. If you touch one thread you send shudders running through all the other threads. We're not just touching the web, we're tearing great holes in it.*

Gerald Durrell

HOME TO A LITTLE LIGHT RELIEF

I HAVE had a bit of trouble lately with my security lights. To be honest, the term security lights gives a false impression. They are not so much a device to light up the cottage for burglars to find a way into my fortress but are useful for me when I come in on a dark night.

We country dwellers do not have street lamps, which is why security lamps are a help. The cottage has three lights. One is at the corner of the Granary, one at the entrance to the garage and one above the porch at the back, which is Upstairs Clare's way into the cottage. Over the years these lights have been more temperamental than a plethora of pop stars. Sometimes they come on for no apparent reason and at other times they ignore our comings and goings. The most recent replacement for a light which insisted on behaving like an actor suffering from stage fright refusing to face the footlights appears to be working well.

Barclay, the rather long dog with the non-distinguished tail and one ear up and one down, causes the two lights at the front of the cottage to come on when he goes out last thing at night for his own inspection of the premises. When he returns to the house after a short interval they should go off. Sometimes they have been known to stay on all the next day.

The wistaria over the garage in summer has its own relationship with its light. A faint breeze can cause a branch to wave in front of the sensor, causing the light to come on in an irritating way. The swallows must enjoy their power to switch on the self-same lamp as they fly in and out of the garage as dusk descends.

The porch light has a mind of its own. It sometimes helps Upstairs Clare to see where to put her key in the lock and at other times appears to enjoy watching her struggling in the dark to find the keyhole.

At the moment all seems to be well with my temperamental trio. They are acting rationally and in the way for which they have been programmed. Like my lights, we are all programmed by our experiences to behave rationally or irrationally. It is good to remember this:

> *Life is too short to bear grudges, too long to fear the darkness. It is best therefore to put one's hand in the hand of God and walk in the light.*

GUARDING AGAINST THE WORST

UPSTAIRS Clare went shopping last Saturday afternoon and bought, on my instructions, a pair of football pads. I had no intention of taking up the game, but I felt they might well solve a problem which has beset me recently: I am the victim of immovable objects which attack me and seem always to catch me on my shins.

I had one such encounter two months before Christmas which took ages to heal, and just before I went to London last month a small table at the Airport, attached to a line of seats, appeared to leap up and hit me, causing me to depart on the plane dripping blood. That one took three weeks to heal, which was an Olympic record.

I had decided that I must protect my shins from further onslaughts from tables, bed ends and the like and get a pair of shinguards.

I wish I had stayed home last Saturday until she returned with the red and black patterned protectors. However, Barclay and I went over to visit Penny and his owner across the road, and a brick in their garden which until then had been perfectly passive and showed no malevolence towards me rose as I stood on it and I pitched forward and the brick removed a portion of my shin skin at the same time.

Across-the-road-Ann was quite happy to run me to Accident and Emergency because her younger son had just been taken there by his father as he (that is Andrew, not David) had fallen off his skateboard and broken his elbow. We Rozel residents lay in Accident and Emergency in opposite beds bemoaning our lot and when I returned home the packet containing the shinguards awaited me.

As I word-process this article I am wearing a large bandage on one leg and a Nike shinguard with a fearsome motif on the other. Neither is visible under my trousers. I am not alone in the Thin Skin Brigade. We clog up the waiting room at A & E. District nurses spend many hours dressing our wounds and warning us of the danger of leg ulcers.

I have passed on some good advice through this column, so I suggest to fellow sufferers: buy some shinguards and sing as you don them the words of the old hymn which begins with Soldiers of Christ arise and put your armour on. The third verse states:

> Leave no unguarded place,
> No weakness of the soul
> Take every virtue, every grace
> And fortify the whole.

NOVEMBER THE FIFTH? IT'S A DOG'S LIFE

'IT is just as well you are not frightened by fireworks,' I said to Barclay the rather long dog with one car up and one down who now shares my life. He was sitting, as is his wont, in the Granary while I was at my desk thinking about November the fifth.

I have had only one dog out of the seven pets who have been my companions who was frightened by the noise of fireworks: Rory, the West Highland terrier, was terrified of both fireworks and thunderstorms. During one storm he escaped from the garden and hid under a table in a neighbour's house whom I really did not know. Finding a small white terrified strange West Highland terrier cowering beneath the tablecloth was almost as unnerving an experience for the lady of the house as the thunderstorm had been for Rory.

When it came to explosions emitting from the gardens of hitherto friendly neighbours, it was more than he could endure. He used to lie under the dining room table and I had to crawl under it to join him in an effort to calm him down. I spent nine tense November the fifths contemplating the table where I had once hidden as a child when my brother and I had turned the table into a robber's den.

Barclay listened while I told him of Rory's fears and reminded him that his girlfriend, Penny, the sheepdog who lives over the road, and William, who lives up the road, are both firework-phobic.

It does seem to me that the explosions are louder than they ever were. Of course, when I used to lie under the table with Rory the noise was slightly muffled, but I have to admit during recent Guy Fawkes nights the explosions reminded me more of the war years in the London Blitz, which I endured, than a happy evening of celebration, which we are all supposed to enjoy.

From ghoulies and ghosties and long-legged
beasties
And things that go bump in the night,
Good Lord deliver us.
Amen

Cornish prayer

TIME TO LOVE ONE ANOTHER

'IS it Methodist soup this week?' A neighbour asked as we went to the parish hall to eat our Friday Lent lunch.

Over the years Lent lunches have played an important part in the life of those of us who attend them. Our lunches consist of soup, cheese, bread and butter and tea or coffee to finish off the feast. The responsibility for making the soup, setting the tables and waiting at table, washing up and putting the parish hall back to rights falls upon the three churches in the parish in turn.

Anglican, Catholic and Methodist soup does not signify the flavour but indicates which denomination is responsible for the soup of the week. Each Friday those of us who observe the fast of Lent do not actually suffer from any sort of starvation because the soup is always delicious, the bread always fresh and the Cheddar cheese is always in plentiful supply. We give a donation to a charity helping those for whom such a meal would, indeed, be a feast.

What then, the outsider may ask, do we gain from what is obviously not a sacrificial meal? The answer is quite simply that we enjoy meeting each other socially. We are not divided by our doctrine but enjoy socialising over our soup. We learn about those in the parish who are sick or are troubled as we talk together. We are glad to remember that the days leading up to Easter were a time when those early disciples met together, ate together and were with Jesus in his last days upon earth.

There was a simplicity about the early Christians and their way of meeting together and it is sad that somehow in the centuries which have passed since that first Holy Week we have somehow distanced ourselves from each other by our inability to come together for worship.

If Lent lunches have taught me one thing over recent years it is that so little divides us and so much unites us that it is high time that we are actually 'Churches Together' without any denominational barriers. Christ's words echo down the years to us today.

A new commandment I give you. Love one another . . . All men will know that you are my disciples If you love one another.

John XIIIv34

71

ALL'S WELL THAT ENDS . . . WITH TOAD

'THERE ought to be a help group called Impulse Buyers Anonymous,' I said to Barclay, the dog with one ear up and one down who was sitting on his cushion in the tailgate of the car.

I specify tailgate because when I once wrote that he was in the boot, someone phoned up to threaten me with the RSPCA!

I am not sure that tailgate is the right description, but Barclay has a tail and he sits at the back of the car in the luggage area. Seated on this occasion in the front seat beside me was Mr Toad, and he was the Impulse Buy.

I had thought for some time, in my idle moments, that it would be a good idea to empty the earth out of the granite trough which was once used to salt a pig and, according to Dulcie my Depend Upon, was called a salter. Having emptied out the earth, I then intended to fill the salter with water and install a water feature.

I had not been inspired by Charlie Dimmock, of TV gardening fame, who single-handedly must have caused the profits of ornamental garden fountain suppliers to soar, but my dream was very simple: to have water pouring gently into the trough in the long hot lazy days of summer.

It was more or less a pipe dream until I saw Mr Toad, complete with tankard and with a pipe coming out of his mouth, in a nearby garden centre. He was elegantly dressed, just like Mr Toad in 'Wind in the Willows', and it was love at first sight.

Love is not cheap, so I had to buy the electrical parts and the other bits and pieces, but plastic cards are a wonderful invention and all that was left was for my dream to become a reality.

Carlos, for whom nothing is any trouble and everything is easily achieved, wired Mr Toad up and soon, with lumps of granite placed here and there, I had a water feature which Charlie Dimmock might well envy.

Normally I am not an impulse buyer, for brought up by a Scottish father with a wealth of moral sayings about saving the pennies to make the pounds, I grew up never dreaming of retail therapy

On a serious note, I have an enormous admiration for those who dedicate their lives to helping people with real addiction problems.

Strengthen those, God, who help others
Who are struggling with temptations which they
Cannot conquer alone.

A PLOT TO PERPETUATE THE PAST

I HEARD a story the other day of a very devoted and very rich couple. The husband took enormous trouble every year thinking of presents for his wife's birthday. The year of the Mercedes convertible and the year of the diamond necklace were highlights of the annual celebration.

One year he found himself somewhat at a loss for a suitable present, as the years had passed and they were getting older, so he decided on a novel gift. He bought a grave plot for his wife and gave her the paperwork on her birthday, making her the proud owner of the grave. She was delighted, although I own I would not have felt the same sense of pleasure!

The following year on her birthday she waited expectantly for her annual gift, but nothing appeared. At last as the day wore on until evening she decided to tackle him.

'Darling, I seem to have no present this year for my birthday,' she said.

'You haven't used the one I gave you last year, darling,' he replied.

I have a grave in the garden here at the cottage in Rozel. I buried Tovey, the dog before Barclay, in the garden up in the shrubbery. I put some stepping stones to lead up to it and there is a circle of stones in the middle of the plot.

This spring I could not walk up to it for the wealth of bluebells which had taken over the path. Nine years ago when Tovey, the dog with the Queen Anne legs, whom readers may remember, died, there were no bluebells in the shrubbery. There were daffodils, primulas and primroses and they have spread as ground cover, but the bluebells are a very welcome addition.

Gravestones remind us of people we have loved. Of course we do not really need such reminders, for those we have loved are always with us. For those with a belief in life after death, we know we will see them again. I have used this Joyce Grenfell quotation before, but it sometimes is a comfort to read it again:

> If I should go before the rest of you
> Break not a flower or inscribe a stone
> Nor when I'm gone speak in a Sunday voice
> But be the usual selves I've always known.
> Weep if you must.
> Parting is hell,
> But life goes on,
> So sing as well.

FLORAL FINERY MADE MY DAY

I HAVE not taken much interest in Valentine's Day for the past 36 years. The man whom I dearly loved was a great romantic and no anniversary passed without his remembering the cards and the flowers. Valentine's Day was no exception, and somewhere among the memorabilia there must be some cards suitably inscribed.

The one anniversary he never chose to remember was the day when we got engaged. He proposed to me on April the First, saying at the time that I would never be able to sue him for breach of promise, for no judge would believe that he was serious in his suggestion that I marry him. As each April the First came round we would laugh over his April Fool Day's joke and were glad that each of us had stuck to our commitment.

Last week on dear Valentines Day a van drew up at the cottage door and I was handed a lovely bunch of freesias by the cheerful deliverer; the card indicated that the sender wished the flowers to be sent anonymously.

It was a lovely surprise and, whoever sent them, thank you very much indeed. I put them in my bedroom because selfishly I wanted to keep the perfume to myself. Also it is colder in there than in the rest of the cottage and they will last longer.

I know very little about the Jewish faith, although I have friends who are faithful followers of that religion. However, when I was thinking of a quotation to end this article I found one in a book which is the Talmud. Checking for a definition of the Talmud, I found that it is the body of Jewish and civil ceremonial law and legend, comprising the Misnah and the Gemara. There are apparently two version of the Talmud, namely the Babylonian, dating from the fifth century, and the earlier Palestinian version. I was glad to learn that and I liked enormously quote I found which sums up for me my Valentine Day flowers:

> When a person does a good deed when he didn't have to,
> God looks down and smiles and says, "For this moment
> alone it was worth creating the world."

GRATEFUL FOR A GOOD COMPANION

FORTY years ago when I wrote my first Saturday Special column I had an Imperial Good Companion portable typewriter. It was a present from my father and I think it cost about seven pounds in the days when seven pounds was a good deal of money. It had followed me round the world and I wrote articles for newspapers and magazines, typed letters and it was in every way a good companion. It did not answer me back and like all good companions was uncritical of my performance. It was occasionally temperamental and the ribbon would jam. The ribbons I favoured were red and black and I could vary the colour of my script according to my whim of the day. Sometimes the little hammers which were the keys stuck up in the air and had to be disentangled for it was before the days of electric typewriters.

Since I got rid of my old faithful good companion I have had a variety of aids to writing and my latest acquisition has taken me into the computer age and I have to own that the experience has been unnerving. My new companion which rejoices in the name of Microsoft Windows 98 makes uncalled-for suggestions to me about what I ought to do next.

It has a terse language of its own. There appears on the screen a range of choices concerning what I ought to do. I can cancel what I have just done, file it, or print it. Add to this it does not always agree with my spelling as some American has programmed it to believe that I would prefer to spell words as those descendants of the Pilgrim Fathers spell. It has underlined the word favour suggesting that I would like to drop the 'u'.

I will not bore my readers with my excursions into the Net for these are early days and I am assured by all my young friends (some as young as six!) that I will grasp it in time.

We live in such a changing world today and the modern technology of Windows 98 is a very long way from the hammer action of my faithful old good Companion. However, the inspiration for these articles over the past 40 years still comes from the same source and that is unchanging. The inspiration is summed up for me in this verse from a hymn by Dora Greenwell.

> I am not skilled to understand,
> What God has willed, what God
> has planned;
> I only know at his right hand
> Stands one who is my Saviour.

NEIGHBOURS FROM HEAVEN

'NOT again. I don't believe it! 'I said in despair as I entered the kitchen one day last month. The kitchen was awash and it was at least the third time in six weeks that the fridge had flooded the kitchen floor.

On this occasion as I drew nearer to the offending piece of modern electrical wizardry I realised that I was accusing the wrong machine of this domestic disaster. The fridge could never have achieved this amount of water. Only the deep freeze could account for this ankle-deep water level.

Barclay, the rather long dog with one ear up and one down who shares my life, rushed into the kitchen in response to my cry of despair. When he saw the pond in the kitchen he retreated hastily. He is not a dog who likes water in any form except for drinking. Anything which threatens to wet him he views with profound distrust. The sea he watches from a distance and this, I suspect, dates back to the time when he chased some ducks on the beach at Rozel into the sea. He was over his paws in sea water when he saw that drowning was facing him so he beat a hasty retreat.

I felt like doing the same on that Sunday morning when faced with clearing up the floor and emptying the deep freeze of its limp contents. Had I really bought five large cartons of delicious Jersey ice cream? I know that Cappuccino is my particular delight but had I really bought three large cartons of it only to find it a milky drink leaking all over the floor of the freezer?

There are times when one cannot cope alone in some emergencies and asking for help is something which I have learned to do. I telephoned my neighbour across the road who lives with her family and Barclay's girlfriend Penny. She came at once armed with a sponge mop and wearing under a sweater some glamorous nightwear. It was after all very early on a Sunday morning.

She removed the semi-frozen vegetables and other items which could be saved and took them over to her deep freeze and then returned and moved the offending deep freeze and I caught the ironing board which was leaning drunkenly on it. It was a hands and knees job as well as a mopping operation before we got the kitchen cleared up.

I was thinking the other day of the commandment of Jesus 'Love your neighbour'. I would like to add a rider to it. There are neighbours from hell and neighbours from heaven. Thank God if yours are from heaven and pray for the ones from hell.

PS: I have bought a new fridge and a new freezer.

CRUMBS OF COMFORT AT BREAKFAST

'YOU'LL have to go to Weight Watchers, Robin,' I said glancing up from my morning reading of the day before's Times.

Regular readers of this column will know that I do the crossword on the day that the paper is delivered and read it the next day while I am having breakfast. Friends who know my habits will also state that I do not always wrap up my comments tactfully, but can go to the jugular, as in the case of my advice to Robin, who was breakfasting with me.

I was having my usual mixed cereal with an apple cut up in it, which I do not particularly enjoy but I am told that fruit should be part of a healthy diet. Robin's breakfast was similar, but his was cereal and fruit in the form of a ball tied to the bird table. He is absolutely addicted to these round delights and gets through one a week on his own. He has become a distinctly round Robin.

The bird table is very close to my kitchen window, so I seldom breakfast alone. Of late I have been forced to abandon my practice of putting loose crumbs on the table because the recent winds have blown them off, providing midnight feasts for Ratty and his friends. This has been unacceptable to me because they have played afterwards in Upstairs Clare's herb tubs, which was very unacceptable to her.

I decided that steps had to be taken, because although the bird table is rat-proof, the garden is not, and I discovered that Rob, a colleague on the paper, is not only a fine writer but also possesses a humane rat trap which he lent me, having first instructed me about how to set it.

I got the hang of it much more quickly than I have mastered the computer. I suppose it is more mechanical than electronic. Before leaving Rob, something did occur to me. 'If one comes into the trap to eat Barclay's tinned dog food and is caught, what do I do then?' I asked.

'You take it somewhere and release it or . . .' his voice trailed away.

I was so glad that equality of the sexes has always been practised in the world of newspapers, but chivalry is also apparent. 'Phone me and I'll come after work,' he said.

I have a little book called The Thank You Book. It contains this quotation:

> Here's to all the little things,
> The done-and-then-forgotten things,
> Those Oh-it's-simply-nothing things
> That make life worth the fight.

LONG DAY'S JOURNEY INTO LIGHT

I KNOW marathon runners are marvellous and I cannot even begin to imagine the pain and suffering they endure as they complete the distance. I watched the London race on television, as I do each year, feeling that I ought to be cheering them on from the comfort of my armchair while wondering afresh what makes them do it.

I know many of them run for charities which they espouse and the money raised increases each year, but many of them could just sign a cheque for the money they raise, and still they do it.

I wished friend and colleague Sue good luck before she left to run her 26 miles 385 yards – or 42.195 kilometres, if you prefer it. I could not watch her on my television screen because she was doing the Boston marathon and finished in very good time and was back at her desk when I handed in my copy a few days later.

Wonderful as marathon runners are, they do not endure the hardships which the tenants of my garage roof suffer on their journey to and from South Africa each year They arrived this year on exactly the same date as last year. I was looking out of the Granary window when father swallow flew in on 17 April. He looked very tired and I was greatly relieved when mother swallow arrived two days later. Perhaps she is a little inclined to dally en route, looking at the view!

I have never been early for engagements but never late until recently, when somehow my expectations about my performance are greater than the reality. I start to prepare in plenty of time but I seem to get into a dawdle mode and by the time I am ready to depart, Grandfather, in the corner, gives me a distinctly long-suffering look. Sometimes he even makes his throat-clearing noise which is preparatory to his striking the hour, which can be very upsetting for that is sometimes the hour when I am due elsewhere.

The welcome I give my swallows is not one which I can pass on to them. How can they know how my heart lifts to see them? How could they guess how I utter a prayer of thanksgiving for their safe return to their summer home?

I know that in life we have heartbreaking times and happy times. My swallows' arrival gives me intense joy and it is an annual bonus.

> *Man was made for joy and woe;*
> *And when this we rightly know,*
> *Thro the world we safely go.*
> *Joy and woe are woven fine,*
> *A clothing for the soul divine.*

William Blake

LADIES WHO LUNCH

BARCLAY, the rather long dog with one ear up and one down, has a friend who lunches out every day.

It could well be argued that this statement is not of overwhelming interest when one considers the great events, international, national or even insular, with which we are concerned. However, the fact that one has a friend who is also a benefactor and who is a lady-who-lunches is of great interest to Barclay, and in a strange way affects me in a different way.

Barclay's Benefactor, like many ladies who lunch, is conscious of her waistline. She therefore cannot consume the whole of the portions which she is given at these well-known eateries, so she asks for a doggie bag. The fact that she has no doggie is of no interest to the establishments whom she favours with her patronage, and the waiters are only too happy to put what she cannot consume into a bag.

These bags vary, for some are specially designed for dogs' delight, with the name of the restaurant printed on them. Others make little baskets of tin foil with a handle which enables his Benefactor to carry them home and put them in her deep-freeze.

Twice a week when we meet at the bowling club she comes and hands over the frozen bags to me and I take them home and put them in my deep-freeze and give the contents to Barclay from time to time. It is on the days when he has peppered steak, or lamb shank, or some other culinary delight that I find my mouth beginning to water. It is not easy for me to settle down to an evening meal of scrambled eggs on soggy toast while Barclay scoffs his chef's delight in the kitchen.

It does not end there, for sometimes a delicious sauce accompanies his meal, and, when later in the evening he gives me a fond lick, I catch a whiff of the sauce provençale and feel a momentary feeling of envy

Of course I know that envy is one of the deadly sins, and although this is a light-hearted article I am aware that temptation happens to most of us at one time or another. We ask God to help us to resist what we are tempted to do and remember that Jesus was tempted even by his friend Peter to do the wrong thing. It is so often friends who tempt us to sin!

Christ's words which he spoke to Peter echo down the years to us at such times:

Get thee behind me, Satan.

JOY IN THE AIR AT EASTER

I SPENT nearly four years living in Malta as a naval chaplain's wife in a flat in a residential home for servicemen and women. The Connaught Home in Floriana is still there as I was delighted to find a few years ago when on a package tour I risked taking the bus to the site just outside Valetta, Malta's capital.

I was fearful, not of the bus journey – although I have to own in my years of living on that devout Roman Catholic island the frequency with which the bus drivers crossed themselves as they stopped and started their vehicles might well have caused me some concern. However, my fear on this recent visit to the Connaught Home was lest it had been turned into a cinema or some such place and the church alongside might have been downgraded into a casino.

My fears were proved groundless for the church was used for occasional concerts and the home housed some of Malta's elderly residents who needed care. That the buildings were still being used for good purposes was a great relief.

I was thinking of my flat and the church opposite our buildings this week as Easter Sunday drew near. The Roman Catholic Archbishop of Malta in our day ruled his people with a kindly but firm rod. He did not approve of any deviation from the strict discipline of the days of Lent. The church bells did not ring out joyously and the altars were draped in purple.

When the Good Friday processions took place the streets were thronged with the faithful and the penitents, who chose to walk hooded, chained and barefoot through the streets, were treated with reverence and respect. By the time Easter Saturday dawned there was joy in the air. The bells rang, the altars were decorated with flowers and the people seemed to be suddenly the happy islanders whom one knew.

I have never known before or since the Easter Message so convincingly acted out. There was gloom and darkness and suddenly on Easter Day there was a burst of gladness as everyone celebrated the Resurrection of Jesus.

Fred Pratt Green has written many hymns which are modern without being sentimentally sugary. One of his Easter hymns begins on a joyous note for Easter morning.

> *This joyful Eastertide,*
> *What need is there for grieving?*
> *Cast all your care aside*
> *And be not unbelieving;*
>
> *(Chorus)*

Come share our Easter joy
That death could not imprison,
Nor any power destroy,
Our Christ is risen.

Then put your trust in Christ
In waking or in sleeping,
His grace on earth sufficed;
He 'll never quite his keeping.

ANXIETIES OF LIFE

'I REALLY don't know which way to turn,' an acquaintance said to me recently. I had stopped to pass the time of day with her and she poured out her troubles as we stood there in the street.

There was nothing I could do but listen and her last sentence summed up how she was feeling. She literally did not know which way to turn for help. I wished I could have told her how to straighten out her marriage difficulties, how to cope with her rebellious children and how to make ends meet in a situation which was getting worse every week. I would have loved to have given her husband a piece of my mind and the children a short, sharp lecture on their total lack of consideration for their mother. I would have liked to have written out a mammoth cheque and to have told my acquaintance that all would now be well.

However, problems are not solved so easily. I had no idea of the other side of the case. I did not know how her husband felt and if her children's behaviour was partly due to the strains and tensions of the relationship.

Paying off the debts is not the answer to every problem, even if one were financially capable of assuming another's burdens.

The problems of life are not easily solved. Life is not a bed of roses for many people. In recent weeks several of my friends have suffered because of the loss of someone who was dear. Others are anxious about relations who are sick and every morning seems to he clouded by anxiety.

We all know the feeling of waking up with the realisation that the day is going to be hard and dread what might happen before nightfall. I have not yet met a person who has escaped from some of the anxieties which life throws up.

There is also a primitive notion that bad things should not happen to good people. How wrong this is. Bad things happen to good and bad people alike. How we react to them is what matters.

God, I cannot see the way forward,
I do now know which way to turn.
Help me to find a way through,
So that I can look back and say,
I survived with Your help.

MEMORIES OF THE MACHINE

MANY years ago now, when I was holidaying in the Outer Hebrides, the powers that be decided that it was time to lay main drains in the island where I was staying with friends.

I was there when The Machine arrived. The Machine was familiar to me, for it was it mechanical digger. However, most of the islanders had not seen such a device. Before the airport was built, there had not been a great deal of coming and going to the mainland.

The arrival of The Machine, pronounced by the Gaelic-speaking islanders with the accent on the first syllable, was declared a public holiday. No one went to work that day for news travelled fast along the little roads from croft to croft and soon there was a trail of pilgrims coming to worship The Machine. They squatted by the side of road and watched with the admiration of men who had dug peat all their lives and for whom mechanical digging was a new science.

As the trench grew along the roadside, they were loud in the praise of the inventor of such a device.

The public holiday stretched over into the next and the next one, for who would want to work while such an operation was being undertaken? As the trench snaked along the narrow road, there was seldom a day without an admiring line sitting on the opposite side watching The Machine.

This week, as I was eating breakfast in the kitchen I heard a humming noise. I walked over to the deep-freeze, fearing that it was about to collapse and reduce the contents of its stomach to moist packages. However, all was well with the Monster. The refrigerator seemed equally content and I rushed through to the boiler house to see if the friend in there who copes with the central heating had had a seizure. All was well there.

I went back to my now cold toast, but glanced out of the kitchen window to see if the noise could be coming from outside. There, in the corner of the daffodil field, a machine was digging a trench. As I stood there I was transported as if on a magic carpet to another island and the smell of peat burning fires filled my nostrils.

I did not give myself a public holiday, for the trench was not going to be very lengthy and The Machine would finish it an hour or two. As I sat down and finished my breakfast, the distant hum of The Machine was a constant reminder of that other island which I love.

In our lives we have places and people we love and even when we are far away from them we have the blessed gift of memory to bring that back to us.

> *A sound, a sigh, a forgotten perfume and we are transported back in time to a place or to a love stored in the vaults of our memories.*

FLOORED BY A VERBAL ONSLAUGHT

'WE will be purposing on the Williams team.' The announcer's voice on Radio 4 on Sunday 22 July woke me up suddenly.

I had been dozing gently, unaware of the British Grand Prix because my thoughts had been focused on who would win the Golf Open, which was being played at the Royal St George club at Sandwich in Kent.

'You will be doing what?' I asked belligerently. 'If you mean you will be *concentrating* on the Williams team and neglecting the other entrants, you might say so, but *purposing* I do not accept.'

Barclay who, since I went away to Bristol for the previous weekend had insisted on having his bed taken through to my bedroom so that he could block any further escape, woke up as I harangued the radio announcer. (Incidentally, he loves his Rozel Harbour boarding house, and the welcome he gets when I leave him makes his pretence that I must never abandon him again worthy of a canine Oscar.)

That Sunday started badly for me with this modern adaptation of the noun 'purpose'. To make it a verb was bad enough, but worse was to come. As I dressed to go to church, I had no idea that my tolerance was to be further stretched.

We were given new hymn books which had been donated by the family of the late and well-loved Alice Laverick. All was going well until the hymn 'Lead us Heavenly Father lead us o'er the world's tempestuous seas' was announced. This is one of my favourite hymns because it was always sung feelingly by sailors at naval services.

It was when we got to the third verse that I decided to sing the original words, for they have been changed in this new edition. My nearest and dearest would never describe me as a candidate for the Singer of the Year competition. I change keys as frequently as some teenagers change their pop idols. However, what I lack in musicality I make up in volume.

The compilers had changed the verse, substituting the word 'ease' for 'cloy' to make it rhyme with a previous amendment. I liked the word cloy, and when I was told afterwards that few people today understood the meaning of the word I said 'Pshaw!' – a word I say well now that I am both eccentric and intolerant.

Here is the unamended verse:

> *Spirit of our God, descending*
> *Fill our hearts with heavenly joy,*
> *Love with every passion blending,*
> *Pleasure that can never cloy;*
> *Thus provided, pardoned, guided,*
> *Nothing can our peace destroy.*

A HOST OF ANGELS HERE ON EARTH

I HAVE never been an authority on angels. I was not brought up to believe that I had a guardian angel who was assigned to me when I was born and who had the task of watching over me for my lifetime. Such a concept was not part of my upbringing, and although it might have been a comforting thought to have had one of these winged creatures perched on the end of my bed, I had to survive without such a protector.

The word angel nowadays is used to describe a quite human wingless person. Nurses are frequently spoken of as angels – and quite rightly. They look after us when we are sick, and do so with cheerfulness and compassion even when the tasks they have to do for us are sometimes unpleasant.

There are other angels who do all sorts of mundane things for others without thought of payment. The mother who collects someone else's children from playgroup or school in an emergency is doing an angel's job. The person who does an elderly person's shopping day after day and drops in for a chat is also doing the work of an angel.

On Remembrance Sunday there will be those who will remember the Angels of Mons. On 26 and 27 August 1914 the 3rd and 4th Divisions of the old Contemptibles were in retreat from the German Army in the Battle of Mons. The losses were horrendous, but it was said by a journalist that the German advance was halted by the miraculous appearance of St George and his angels with flaming swords.

Whether this was a flight of the journalist's imagination or really some miraculous flight of angels has never been established, but what is certain is that a monumental attack was halted. Subsequently, the Angels of Mons became a phrase and fable of the history of the time.

There is a hymn written by Henry Burton, who lived from 1840 to 1930. It contains these words:

> *But his angels here are human, not the shining hosts above.*
> *And the drumbeats of his army are the heartbeats of our*
> *love.*

FOR WHEN THE LADY VANISHES

I SHOULD have liked so much to have met Dorothy Sayers. I have read most of her detective stories. She did not suffer, as modern thriller writers do, from publishers choosing to attract readers with lurid pictures on the dust jacket or on the cover of the paperback.

A picture of a murderer standing over a victim with blood pouring out of a knife wound with the hilt of the weapon protruding would not instantly attract me to read that book. On reflection, I might well never have read P D James, one of the most skilful detective writers of today, if I had not overcome my aversion to some of the illustrative covers on her books.

I am longing to sit down and read 'Dorothy L Sayers: Her Life and Soul', by Barbara Reynolds, which was given to me for Christmas. It looks fascinating, and on the front cover there is a portrait of Sayers. The foreword is by P D James, who wrote that this new book brings the writer and the woman alive in a way that no previous author has achieved.

Dorothy Sayers lived finally with two men in her life: her husband and Lord Peter Wimsey, the detective in her books whose character was rather different from some of the rather more plebeian characters in today's TV detective soaps!

Dorothy Sayers had another side to her. 'The Man Born To Be King' was one of the most moving accounts of Christ's life and is described as 'a great evangelistic undertaking, an unprecedented achievement in religious education and one which has never been equalled'.

I should have liked to meet this multi-faceted woman. As an academic she had a tempestuous love life after Oxford. The birth of an illegitimate child to a woman who was a devout Anglo-Catholic has been well reported. She was born in 1893 and died in 1957 after a Christmas shopping trip to London. Tired after her day out, she went home and after feeding her cats dropped dead at the foot of the stairs.

She wrote a poem called 'Hymn in Contemplation of Sudden Death' when she was still at Oxford. I think that it is curiously comforting for those who have unexpectedly lost someone they love in just such a way.

> *Lord, if this night my journey end*
> *I thank thee first for many a friend,*
> *The sturdy and unquestioned piers*
> *That run beneath my bridge of years.*
>
> *And next for all the love I gave*
> *To things and men this side the grave.*
> *Wisely or not, since I can prove*
> *There is always much good in love.*
>
> *Next for the power thou gavest me*
> *To view the world mirthfully.*
> *For laughter, Paraclete of pain*
> *Like April sun across the rain.*

HELP AT HAND FOR TRIP DOWN THE AISLE

I AM not supermarket shopping material. Every so often I set forth determined to do what is called a 'big shop' by my friends. These friends go forth armed with lists and return with countless plastic bags stuffed to the brim in the boot of their cars. Once home, they unload their booty and systematically stow the contents of the bags into cupboards, pantries, deep freezers or whichever place is the ultimate destination for their endeavours.

As a reward for their efforts, from the store which they favour they either get double divvy points or coupons which have to be stuck in books giving a discount when the magic time comes, or they may even have a feeling of great complacency because as well as all these coupons and dividend benefits, their mammoth shopping has brought them two-for-the-price-of one articles which are bargains well spotted.

My own sorties are very different. For one thing, the list is almost always left on the kitchen table and I have to try to remember what it was I so badly needed. My mind runs along curious lines. I am irresistibly drawn to the kitchen and toilet roll counters. I fill the trolley with these items in a frantic effort to remember what else I need.

I get panic-stricken at the frozen ready-meal counter and plump for fish pie. Admiral's Pie, Captain's Pie and even Ocean Pie draw me like nautical magnets. I do not believe there is any difference between them other than rank, though Ocean Pie is obviously a lower-deck concoction with no mention of the sailors who are contained in the recipe. The admirals and the captains, on the hand, are mentioned as befits their rank.

After the frozen food section I escape to the paying-out till embarrassed by the lack of imagination which my purchases proclaim. I think it is because faced with an enormous choice, I freeze in the aisles and simply escape from the supermarket maze into which I have stumbled.

In life we are often faced with temptations and we have to make choices. Sometimes we do not know what to do and at such times we must pray to God for help.

> Prayer: God, sometimes I don't know which way to turn. Life is so difficult. Help me choose the right path, and if I choose the wrong one give me strength to find my way home.

THE RICH REWARDS OF TOTAL TEAMWORK

THE house where I spent the very early years of my life was near Pittodrie. That statement will mean little or nothing to those people who are not Scottish and know nothing of the football grounds where Scottish teams play. Pittodrie was then – and still is, I imagine – the home of Aberdeen Football Club.

Every Saturday afternoon when there was a home match being played, the street where I lived was a seething mass of cloth caps as supporters thronged to the stadium to cheer the Dons, which is the name of my native city's football team. The supporters were disgorged from the tramcars. Few, if any, came by motor car, and buses brought the opposing team's supporters to the ground.

Although it was a long time ago, I can still remember thinking, when the Dons were playing at home, that I could have walked on the heads of the men as they made their way to Pittodrie, so close-packed was the crowd. Traffic was held up until the start of play, and again it was stopped when the crowd emerged, singing or silent at the end of the game, depending upon whether the Dons had won or lost.

Some football supporters certainly got drunk in those far-off days. They walked very unsteadily home after the match and there were a few fights with those who had supported the opposing team. I do not remember people getting stabbed to death or beaten senseless in the city's streets, but tabloid journalism was not yet born to sensationalise such episodes, nor were there TV cameras to highlight the ugly scenes.

I think it is good to support a team, whether it be a major league or simply a school team or club. Loyalty to a club is good if the aims of the club are worthwhile. It is, I am told, more difficult to get youngsters to play team games than it was a decade or two ago. They are happy to support a team and parents know only too well the high cost of buying the football strips of a major club which their young people support. They like to identify with their chosen team but are not so willing to play for their school or club.

When it comes to supporting God's team it is well to remember this quotation:

God wants players as well as prayers in His team.

THE GAMES PEOPLE PLAY

'WHICH game do you think is most calculated to make you lose your temper?'

The person who asked the question was sitting with me having a quiet cup of coffee and the subject of games and tempers somehow came up. I spent a little while thinking before answering, and asked if it had to be based on personal playing experience.

It would he difficult for me to say how I felt about playing rugby because the game had never been one of my pastimes. In my day it was not deemed to be a women's game, but now there seem to be no holds barred and women play most sports which men enjoy.

Upstairs Clare, who shares the cottage with me and with Barclay, the rather long dog with one ear up and one down, plays a game called touch rugby. I imagine it is a gentler form of the familiar game played with the oval ball, but Upstairs Clare comes back from matches looking as if she has been in the odd scrum or two!

To revert to the subject under discussion, I have played hockey, tennis, badminton, netball, snooker, golf, croquet, bowls and pétanque in my day. I think croquet has been the only one which has caused me to think nasty thoughts about my opponents. To have your ball knocked miles across the lawn just as it was about to go through the last hoop is an experience which causes the most even-tempered person to feel a certain amount of animosity. I have seen apparently civilised people stamp their feet, sulk, throw their mallets, stamp off the pitch and threaten never to play the wretched game again.

The principle of bowls and pétanque is not too different from croquet: one's opponents are bent on destruction and it takes a certain amount of self-control not to show one's feelings when disaster in the form of a carefully aimed wood destroys the defensive strategy which had been carefully constructed.

I am a great believer in people playing games. It teaches youngsters to become part of a team and to learn self-control. I believe God must like a generous winner and a good loser.

I am sometimes asked by my bowling friends to find a prayer for the bowling fraternity. I have not found one yet, but I offer up this little petition for those on the rink who occasionally ask the Lord to help them when things seem to be going wrong!

> *I ask not Lord for wealth or fame,*
> *I ask not for a cup with my name,*
> *But if You could with a Divine whack*
> *Sometimes help my wood to hit the jack.*

HISTORY COMES TO THE BOIL

I ALWAYS take my Percolator when I go on holiday. For those who know of my caffeine addiction this will not be a surprise, although most of my closest friends who know of the collection of cafétières which decorate my kitchen would be surprised at the mention of a percolator.

However, the Percolator is different from a cafétière because it is my nickname for my friend and holiday companion Bennie. Her task on our travels is to absorb the relevant historical, geographical and cultural information and then, having assimilated the facts, give me a précis of the knowledge she has painfully acquired. This necessitates much reading and studying on her part before we embark on some adventure and requires absolutely no effort for me.

The main reason for this delegation of authority is because I am geographically and historically illiterate, and somehow culture has also passed me by. I can now, in the twilight years, absorb a small amount which the Percolator pours into my diminished brain and I am happy.

Having just returned from a delightful trip to Prague and then on the River Elbe up to Berlin through all the delights of Dresden,

Meissen and Wittenburg, I can pass on some knowledge which I have gained.

I especially enjoyed seeing the wonderful art collection in the Zwinger Palace in Dresden, which houses Raphael's Sistine Madonna in the Old Masters' Gallery. The two little cherubs in the painting have become famous in their own right, for they are frequently portrayed on postcards and souvenirs of the city.

I have a ticket for the gallery on my desk and the putti are smiling up at me as I write. Putti is the plural of putto, which is a representation of a naked child, especially a cherub or a cupid in Italian Renaissance art. That last piece of information I owe entirely to the Percolator!

I came into my own in Wittenburg, for our RE teacher grounded us firmly in the story of Martin Luther, who in 1571 was excommunicated at the Diet of Worms for preaching against the sale of indulgences and other misdeeds of the Roman Catholic Church. The door of the church in Wittenburg where he nailed his 95 articles is a tourist attraction of considerable importance. Luther founded the Protestant church and today, as Roman Catholics and Protestants move closer together, we rejoice in what we have in common.

A safe stronghold our God is still
As trusty shield and weapon:
He'll help us from all the ill
That hath us now o'ertaken.

Luther

REACHING FOR THE SKY

I WENT to the Air Display this month. To be honest I did not exactly go to it but watched it in great comfort from the balcony belonging to two of my friends.

I had staying with me at the time an old Wren officer friend who had expressed a desire to see the latest thing in aircraft. Her interest was greater than mine for she had been in charge of maintaining radios in naval aircraft during the 1939 war while I was merely on the administrative side.

I have to own that I have a curious memory blank when it comes to distinguishing one aircraft from another, which is unfortunate to say the least as my one and only beloved son is an aircraft buff, and having a mother who is unable to distinguish between Concorde and a Dakota is an embarrassment to him.

Be that is it may, for the very first time I watched the air display and marvelled at the Red Arrows performing complex manoeuvres in the sky. I held my breath when they broke formation and passed within what appeared to be inches of each other at breakneck speed.

Chided by my friends over cup of tea between flying episodes about it being my first sight of Jersey's great air attraction, I admitted that it was not my first visit to an air show. In the far distant past as a small child I had been taken to the beach at Aberdeen to witness a superb example of bombing accuracy during an air show (I think they called it an air circus) when a clown in an Austin Seven was bombed with a bag of flour which the pilot threw over the side of his open plane. It was a far cry from the technology which guides bombers to their targets today but that early pilot no doubt subsequently served in the RAF.

Later in life I survived the London blitz, dodging real bombs which were very unlike the flour-bag bombing of those far-off days.

It is good that we, as an Island, give generously to the RAF Benevolent Fund for we owe the survivors and their dependents so much. God loves a cheerful giver so we must give generously.

Do not despair for Johnny head-in-air;
He sleeps as sound
As Johnny underground.
Better by far
For Johnny-the-bright-star
To keep your head And see his children fed.

Pudney

IF YOU WANT TO GET AHEAD, GET A PSALM

WHAT do you do if a completely strange man offers to show you his tattoos?

This is not just an academic question but happened to a friend who lives in Surrey. She owns a rather pleasant ground-floor flat in an Edwardian house, and a studio and two other flats are rented. The other night, she told me on the telephone, a stranger rang her doorbell and introduced himself as the new tenant in the studio flat. He told her that he was in security but also did a bit of acting, and he had come to say that if ever she needed help, he was on hand. Touched by his offer and interested in the acting aspect of his career, she asked him what was his particular field. Apparently he had been in a television programme because of his unusual tattoos.

At this point she admitted to me that she felt a certain apprehension. In my day, the suggestion that one might like to come up and see someone's etchings was a prelude to being in a situation from which it might be difficult to extricate oneself. Tattoos would obviously present a greater problem.

'Would you like to see the tattoos?' asked her shaven-headed new neighbour. There are invitations which are easy to refuse and some are more difficult. However, before she could decide how to refuse without offending him, he suggested she might like to look at the one on his head. He bent down and there, clearly tattooed on his shaven head, was the whole of the 23rd Psalm! Apparently it had been done when he was a member of a church youth club.

I asked her which version it was of the well known shepherd Psalm, but she had been too taken aback to study the script carefully.

Sitting at my desk thinking of the incident, I turned up the anthology of Psalms which someone gave me recently. I found the one translated from a version by a Japanese woman. I have not space to quote the whole of it, but will save some for another Special.

> *The Lord is my Pace-setter, I shall not rush;*
> *He makes me stop and rest for quiet intervals.*
> *He provides me with images of stillness, which restore*
> *My serenity;*
> *He leads me in ways of efficiency through calmness of*
> *mind,*
> *And his guidance is peace.*
> *Even though I have a great many things to accomplish*
> *each day,*
> *I will not fret, for His presence is here.*

Toki Miyashina

A CLASSIC COLOSSAL CLEAN-UP

'I'M going to have a Roman orgy. You could all come and bring your own grapes.'

I have to admit that there was a hushed silence in the newsroom of our distinguished evening paper when I proffered the invitation. Yet when they had absorbed the offer one wit suggested that only a Scot would invite anyone to an orgy with the proviso to bring their own grapes!

I had been discussing the shower that I was having installed in my bathroom when the subject of Roman orgies came up. The shower catalogue described the one I had chosen as a Roman Classic Colossus, and it was much larger than the usual box shower, having no door but a sort of walk-in entrance.

The sellers of this magnificent bathroom fixture had mentioned that a previous Member of the States who had served his Island and parish well and whose initials were the same as JR in Dallas might like to show me the one which he and his wife had had fitted before I took the plunge, so to speak. I telephoned and asked if I might invite myself round, and was given coffee as well as a personal view of their Roman Colossus. I did not take the opportunity of a personal test, for they were enthusiastic about their acquisition and I preferred the offer of coffee to a mid-morning splash.

Having opted for the shower, I have been fascinated by the way the workforce have set about their business. My own plumber regretted giving me his mobile number, for as clerk of works I had frequent telephone conferences with him. Plumbers, tilers, my electrician, carpet fitter and builder all set to stripping my bathroom ready for the new pieces of equipment.

I was sad that the dairy farmers were cutting down, for my old green bath would have looked environmentally friendly as a cattle watering place, but it had to go to Bellozanne in pieces.

The finished bathroom is wonderful. I even have a seat in the shower so that I can dally for a while to consider what a fortunate person I am to have enough money to enjoy such luxury.

I have decided against any orgies, for the founder of Methodism, John Wesley, would not have approved of such excesses. He would have approved of the shower, however, for he wrote the following in his 93rd sermon. He had a vast collection of sermons of which every Methodist preacher had to read and digest 44. I know I did it!

> *Let it be observed that slovenliness is no part of religion;*
> *that neither this nor any text of Scripture condemns*
> *neatness of apparel. Certainly this is a duty not a sin.*
> *Cleanliness is indeed next to godliness.*

MAKING IT BETTER WITH A KISS

THE little girl who was running down the hill past my cottage fell. She picked herself up, howling loudly, and her mother, who was only a few steps behind, rushed and picked her up.

From the window I could observe the scene. The child's knees were unmarked but the fall had frightened her and the sobs were heart-rending. I could hear them through the secondary double-glazed windows, which do cut out a great deal of the noise of the passing traffic in the little road in which my cottage stands.

The mother knelt down and cradled the child and looked to see what sort of damage had been done. I was ready with the first aid kit, had the casualty merited it. However, I thought I would go out without the little case, which contains the plasters, micro-film sterile dressings and the like, lest we were not needed.

As I turned the corner of the garage I heard a time-honoured phrase being spoken. 'Look. Mummy will kiss it better.' In a moment the sobbing ceased and the crisis was over.

I was transported back as I stood watching them walk down the valley to my own childhood, when my mother had a great belief in the curative powers of a kiss. Never demonstrative by nature, she, nevertheless, was always on hand to kiss the offending damaged part of a small body, although further treatment occasionally followed.

The security of being swept up in the comfort of her arms and her apparent belief in the curative powers of a kiss were never failing.

I have to own that the further treatment was far less pleasant. Anyone who remembers iodine being dabbed onto an open cut will shiver with me as they remember the excruciating pain. The bottle stood in the medicine cupboard of our family home and it was coloured blue with a serrated edge lest someone drank it in the dark in error. Certainly one would not drink it intentionally.

I carried on the tradition, as most mothers do, and kissed grazed knees better when my own son fell and hurt himself. How often we wish we could kiss the hurts of those we love better when much worse tragedies than grazed knees befall them. Loving those who are in pain is certainly the first step we must take in any healing process.

Christ said when he was preaching:

Love suffers long and is kind.

SHELLFISH: THE BOTTOM LINE

THE term 'bottoms up' came to me when I was on holiday this year in France. I was driving at the time across the Passage du Gois, which links Beauvoir-sur-Mer to the Ile de Noirmoutier.

I own that I was driving somewhat nervously along the causeway, which was described on the map as *route practicable à basse mer*. There was, just a few miles down the road, a perfectly adequate bridge which had been constructed to prevent those of us of a nervous disposition from risking floating out into the Bay of Bourgneuf. However, my holiday companion was determined to take our lives and my brand new car along the road – which was passable only at low tide – because she wished to see those intrepid souls who go low-water fishing.

It was an astonishing sight as we went, for on both sides of the causeway there were hundreds of bottoms, the owners of which were intent on getting all sorts of shellfish for their culinary delight. Few raised their heads as we passed by. Not only was bottoms up the order of the day, but the old bingo call 'eyes down' also came to my mind as I noted their dedication to their task.

There were refuges consisting of little huts on stilts with ladders up which one could climb while presumably watching one's vehicle being washed out to sea, or, worse, the unwary fisherman or woman drowning in pursuit of a bucketful of prawns.

Low-water fishing is familiar to me but merely as a spectator sport. I have friends who are expert low-water fishers, and they frequently show me their catch of a pint or two of prawns from their own secret rock pool. They never divulge where they find their treasure lest others, hearing of it, will beat them to their favoured spot at the next low tide.

As I remembered this week the low-water fisherfolk of the Passage du Gois, I thought how intent they were upon their pursuit of their prey. It would not be difficult for them to fail to note the rising tide and not see the rising waters lapping round their ankles.

We do not always see the danger which can overtake us either in a physical situation or in a moral one.

> Help us, Father, to see the hidden danger, and help us find
> the way which leads to the safety of Your love.

PATTERNS OF BEHAVIOUR

'IF he doesn't get his toast and Marmite last thing at night he goes berserk.'

I caught this snatch of conversation as I passed two women shoppers on one of my rare trips to St Helier. I would have dearly loved to have turned round and followed them to hear the rest of the conversation because my curiosity was roused. Who was it who went berserk if denied their nightly Marmite fix? Could it be a husband or a partner who looked forward all evening to this treat? On the other hand, it might be a child for whom a night-time story was not so important as the toastie treat. It might even be a dog for whom the conventional canine biscuit had been rejected in favour of the more tasty treat!

As I walked along, I found myself intrigued by my conjectures. Then I turned my mind to just how berserk the person or animal went. Were there wild scenes in the kitchen or bedroom when, deprived of the snack before sleep, crockery was flung across the work surfaces or dressing table ornaments were hurtled onto the fitted bedroom carpet?

The word berserk, after all, indicates total lack of control, and while most people can feel a mild irritation or even rage at a departure from tradition, to go berserk is something yet again.

People's patterns of behaviour are different. For the person with an obsessive personality it is extremely difficult to encompass any sort of change of routine. One can see the beginnings of it in childhood when the toddler must have his toys in exactly the same place and his clothes must be put on in a certain order.

The carefree non-obsessive people of the world are so much more fortunate than those whose personalities impose upon them certain ritualistic behaviour patterns. When a habit takes over our lives then we have to ask ourselves whether we are the masters of our behaviour or the servants of it. Some habits are good and help us to control our lives. Others are harmful and have to be seen as such.

I have quoted this Wayside pulpit verse before, but I think it is apt:

> *Every time I pass this church I pay a little visit so when*
> *I'm carried in last the Lord won't say, 'Who is it?'*

AT THE COURT OF PRINCE KIKI

'NOUS *avons perdu nos coeurs à Kiki Montfort, le prince des frontons,'* I said to the pensionaires at the auberge in the foothills of the Pyrenées where I spent an idyllic three-week holiday last month.

Readers of this column may recall that some years ago after spending time in the Haut Pyrenées near Lourdes I wrote of my undying affection for a man who owned a restaurant up in the mountains who could cook like an angel. Since that time colleagues at the newspaper have chided me about my 'holiday romance' – which I have to own was no more than an admiration for the man who could cook on an open grill the most delectable dishes and seemed to be oblivious of either the heat from the fire or the 100-degree summer temperature which we then endured.

Kiki Montfort was definitely in the same class. I and Bennie, my intrepid holiday companion, who had shared the Lourdes experience, were determined to go to see Kiki Montfort. His name was plastered on every advertisement. There were banners across the road at Cambo Le Bains, our nearest little town, telling us when we could see *le prince,* and on the last day of July we went to the *fronton* at St Pee-sur-Nivelle to see him.

Lest I have readers who do not know what a *fronton* is, and I did not know myself what it was until last month, let me explain. A *fronton* is a stone wall about the height of the gable end of a house on which a black line about three feet up from the bottom is painted. Against the *fronton* Basque people and Spaniards play outdoor pelota.

Space does not permit me to explain the rules of this game, but it is played sometimes with bare hands, sometimes with things like knuckledusters, but the champions like Kiki Montfort play with the chistera, a basketlike device fastened to the hand. It was once more about 100 degrees F and Kiki and the other five professionals played for an hour with frequent breaks to have water poured over them. Pelota is one of the fastest games I have ever seen played. Kiki was well named. He was indeed *le prince des frontons.*

To achieve a high standard in any sport or indeed to be successful in life we have to have an inner strength and a commitment. The Olympic Games show that to perfection, and in the same way anyone who wants to succeed in life has to have a determination not to be beaten, however difficult the task.

> *That which is within us is stronger than that which is without.*

ALL THE RAGE

THIS new disease which has been recently identified I have been aware of for many years. Indeed, I have suffered from it but have so far managed to live with it. Recent cases which have been reported in the press and on television news bulletins have made me realise that the symptoms are exactly those from which I have suffered for years.

The disease now has a name. It is called Road Rage.

It afflicts motorists who quite suddenly have had enough of the driver of the car in front or in the car behind.

I have felt the onset of Road Rage but I have practised rigid self-control and have never, to date, leapt out of my own vehicle and abused, either verbally or physically, the other motorist. However, I have felt like it!

Bennie, the friend who puts up with me on holiday, coined the name 'porpoise' for the motorist who insists on driving too close behind one's car. The name comes, of course, from 'Alice in Wonderland' and refers to the conversation which the whiting had with the snail when he found the porpoise behind him in the line treading on his tail.

Drivers who insist on getting up one's exhaust are descended, without a doubt, from the porpoise!

Road Rage is riot the only rage which I stifled over the years. Queue Rage has hit me badly at times when someone has jumped the queue al the checkout or in the theatre, and it has taken me all my time to remember about loving one's neighbour even if that neighbour is a queue jumper extraordinaire.

Meal Rage was another of the diseases which I suffered from in the days when I was head cook and bottle washer for my family. The individual members would be waiting for the meal to lie ready and the moment that it was on the table they would all vanish. It was as if a silent whistle had sounded and they all disappeared on urgent business while I stood waiting, serving spoon in hand, watching the food cool while I got hot with rage.

> *God You know how impatient we get, and how sometimes*
> *we get angry with those we love and even with those we*
> *do not even know. Forgive us and strengthen us.*

GROWING PAINS

I HAVE been watching the *Magnolia stellata* with some anxiety. It had been smothered under a mahonia, which was denying it the light it needed, so we moved it. Well, to be more accurate, Fernando, who helps me in the garden, moved it while I supervised.

I have become a good supervisor of late and can lean on a spade and give advice without feeling guilty about my non-active participation. The days of spending four hours, sickle in hand, cutting the grass bank behind the shrubbery have gone. To be realistic, one no longer sees the grass bank which used to be alive with daffodils in the spring because the shrubbery has provided a very attractive, very high, variegated curtain. I had not realised when I planted the shrubs 30 years ago that one day they would be 15 ft high!

The funniest shrubs are the three pittosporum which now

resemble trees in a forest. I planted them so that I could pick the odd branch or two to put in with a vase of flowers. The possibility of picking any of their branches is certainly now too remote. Only a lumberjack with crampons could shin up the pittosporum trees.

Good gardeners know where to plant shrubs or trees so that in 30 years they will still be sympathetic additions to the garden. Good nurserymen should warn the novice gardener of the rate of growth and space that will be needed for their purchases.

In a way, shrubs and trees are a little like children. Many parents are surprised when they see the physical changes which take place as their son or daughter reaches maturity. Who would have thought that the sweet little boy in the Babygrow would one day be the six-foot giant with the dreadlocks and earrings? Or who would have, in their wildest dreams, imagined that the beautiful chubby, golden-haired little girl would become the painfully thin red-headed teenager with rings in each nostril who insists on wearing thick boots with every outfit?

Children grow up and mature and we do well to wait patiently for that time. Parents, like gardeners, have to be extremely patient. They have much in common. Watching plants and children grow can be rewarding or heartbreaking.

> *Children need love, especially when they do not deserve it.*
> *(In bringing up children spend half as much money and*
> *twice as much time.)*

H S Hulbert

OLD FOLK IN THE ATTIC

GETTING up to the loft to see if it was there was no easy task. I have not got, as I have mentioned in this column before, a loft ladder of the type which one pulls down with a hook, making the ascent an easy and straightforward matter. I have a trapdoor in the Granary and a ladder in the garage. The ladder in the garage is extremely heavy and I have to carry that and line it up beneath the access roof trapdoor. All this takes time. And then, having ascended the ladder, I have to balance the trapdoor for a few moments on my head while I dislodge it.

I have carried out this operation for the past 15 years, but I cannot put my hand on my heart and say that it is my favourite exercise.

However, the other week I was wondering what had happened to a wedding present which seemed to be missing. It had never really been used much, because the article in question went out of fashion. In my mother's day, everyone had one, and in my family home afternoon tea would not have been thought complete without one. Just as one had scones, Victoria sponge cake and shortbread for tea, one also had a cakestand on which to mount these goodies.

Mother's was a mahogany three-tier affair which folded down when not in use. I was given a similar object and I thought it was in the loft. I had used it in the heady days when my friends ate fattening and delicious tea. The cakestand was handed round, and everyone tucked in without a thought of the calories which they were consuming.

Alas, those happy days have gone, and so has the cakestand. Did it disappear in the night? Perhaps it was stolen during one of our many moves from place to place. Wherever it has gone, I doubt if it will be put to good use, for like so many other objects of another age it has outlived its usefulness.

It is perfectly normal and proper that things do go out of fashion because they are no longer thought to be of use. The saddest thing is when this philosophy is extended to people. Occasionally it is said of someone that 'he is past his sell-by date'. The idiom of the supermarket is used to describe someone who appears to be no longer of use to the community. If a community has no use for those who have grown old in its service, there is something wrong with our society.

I have seen heartbroken old people whose family no longer visit them or care for them. They have outlived their usefulness to the family. They have been metaphorically put in the loft.

I found in the Oxford Book of Prayers this one, written by a young Ghanaian Christian.

> *Lord, keep my parents in your love. Lord bless them, and keep them. Lord, please let me have money and strength and keep my parents for many more years so that I can take care of them.*

IT'S A DOG'S LIFE – IF YOU ARE LUCKY

'I FOUND a letter which I had cut out from The Times which I thought might interest you,' I said to Barclay, the rather long dog with one ear up and one down who shares my life.

He was sound asleep on the settee in the sitting room. He has what people nowadays call a 'throw' on the settee and he likes to jump from a recumbent position onto the back of the settee, where he assumes the role of sentry on duty and no one comes down the valley without his alerting me of their passing. The Vallée de Rozel is the best-guarded area in the parish, if not in the whole Island! In these days of having to install security lights and alarms, Barclay is worth his weight in hundreds of tins of his favourite dog food as a member of my personal Securicor firm.

Sometimes I have to interrupt his slumbers or his sentry duty to get him to listen to me. He understands a great number of words, but on other occasions he has to provide a listening ear so that I can read something in order that I can hear how it sounds.

Naturally I could read it quietly in the Granary which was named after my late beloved mother, who was known as Gran to all of us. She had always regretted that I had no west window in the cottage when she lived the last five years of her life with me, and as the cottage walls were too thick to provide such an indulgence, I had to wait until after her death to do the rather major addition to the Granary.

Be that as it may, I must return to the letter from The Times which I read to Barclay. I quote it in full. A fax was sent to a hotelier in the French Pyrenées asking if the guest's dog would be allowed to stay in the hotel. The reply was to this effect: 'I have been a hotelier for 25 years. I have never seen a dog steal an ashtray or a spoon, or burn the sheets with a cigarette. I never had to call the police for a dog being drunk and disorderly and a dog has never been rude to the staff. That's the reason why I welcome dogs.

'PS. You, too, are welcome should you decide to accompany your dog.'

The name of the hotelier was not printed.

Barclay listened with interest and I went through to the Granary to think of the moral to this tale. It is this:

> It is sometimes said that people behave like animals. On the whole, animals behave better than the lawless immoral, Godless members of today's society.

THE ART OF LISTENING

THE valley was swept absolutely clean two weeks ago in preparation for more roadworks. We valley dwellers had been warned well in advance of the intention of the Public Services Department, but the ominous sounding notice about the road closure struck the usual sort of dismay in my heart. I do not like it when I am unsure about whether I will be able to get out of the cottage with ease, and I viewed the early morning appearance of the big yellow monster with misgiving.

It was followed by a team of men in luminous jackets armed with brushes as it lumbered up and down the valley. It had, protruding from its sides, brushes, rather like fins, which dealt with the leaves in the ditches with comparative case.

As it went it flashed a yellow light and I found myself mesmerised by its progress. I had plenty to do in the Granary, named after my Gran, my beloved mother, and not denoting that the room had once been a grain store, but I continued to lean on the window ledge watching the monster and its attendants instead of getting down to work. They looked happy as they swept the road.

As the new year begins, some people have found themselves in the retirement zone. They admit that not going to the workplace where they have spent the best part of their lives has been an unnerving experience. They miss the companionship of their fellow workmates, and the routine of leaving home and returning at the end of the day is suddenly missing.

One man spoke to me recently about the change in his life now that he was retired. The emptiness which he was now experiencing was a totally new experience and he wanted to know if I had any suggestions about how he might fill the seven hours which had suddenly become an empty period of his life. 'Don't suggest I do any good works,' he said, indicating by the belligerence of his tone that this had been a frequent suggestion.

I murmured something about taking up new hobbies, new sports or new interests. These suggestions fell on deaf ears, but then he made a very revealing remark. 'She doesn't really like having me round the house,' he said abruptly and walked away.

People frequently reveal the real source of their worry at the end of a conversation. It is, therefore, always worth waiting and listening patiently.

Teach me God the skill of listening for I cannot hear if I am talking.

GETTING THE MESSAGE ACROSS

A YARD of ale is the amount of beer (typically two to three pints) held by a narrow glass approximately one yard long. I was looking up the definition of a yard of ale because I received a Christmas present which was a measurement of something to which I am addicted.

Lest there are those readers still suffering from Hogmanay hangovers, I might perhaps make my opening two sentences more clear.

I did not receive a yard of ale as a Christmas present, but I received a foot of fudge from my friend Lorna, who knows about my addiction. The fudge was measured out in the form of a ruler and indeed had the words 'skool ruler for fudgeaholics' written on it. To all intents and purposes, it looks exactly like the one I owned when I attended that distinguished Scottish emporium of learning for girls and the ruler had several pithy sayings written on its sides. One side was inscribed 'School's a drudge, eat more fudge' and on the other side the familiar warning 'This ruler belongs to ME'.

I smiled when I read the warning written on the ruler daring anyone else to touch it. All my school books and pencil cases were similarly adorned, with my name and address usually ending the address with Scotland, British Isles, Europe, and the World, so that there should be no doubt about the name and address of the owner.

There has been a tendency in recent years for manufacturers of goods to mark their products with their names. I can remember refusing to buy a golf bag which had Dunlop in huge white letters on its side. My question to the golf professional asking how much I would get for advertising the maker was not taken seriously.

Years later, sports clothing and ordinary garments were adorned with the makers' names so that everyone would know which fashion house the wearer supported. I have a long-sleeved T-shirt which has the word Naff on a label at the back. Many friends have suggested I am wearing it inside out.

Whether we sport the name of some fashion designer or have our own names on our possessions matters little. In relationships, possessive love between two people is not healthy – we have to learn to love others as God loves us.

> *Only he who knows God knows what love is; it is not the other way round.*

Dietrich Bonhoeffer

WANTED: ROOM TO MANOEUVRE

THEY arrived on 17 April looking slightly weary after the journey. They were not exactly jetlagged, for they did not travel by plane but came under their own steam from southern Africa.

They know the route well and they need no road map once they hit Jersey, for they always make straight for the cottage, do a lap of honour and fly into the garage to inspect their summer quarters.

They are the least demanding of guests, for they ask no more of me, their summer landlady, than I leave my car out of the garage for six months. To be quite truthful, they have never asked me to vacate the garage, but there are no swallow lavatory facilities laid on and having to clean the car daily is more than I can undertake.

While on the subject of car cleaning, I stopped off at the car wash in St Mary last week and managed, with difficulty, to perform all the necessary functions prior to the car's ablutions.

I pressed the button which makes the wing mirrors fold into the side of the car, checked that all the windows were closed, removed Barclay, the rather long dog with one ear up and one down who shares my life, and pushed the switch which turns on the water.

Half-way through the operation I noticed that I had forgotten to put the aerial down. Luckily, a very well known St Mary resident, who was obviously a favoured customer, came over for a chat, and when I pointed out that I was about to have my aerial bent in half she called out to one of the garage men and between the washing and drying programme he rushed in and pushed down the aerial.

It's not what you know, it's who you know, I thought, as I said thank you to Jersey's most senior woman Jurat.

To go back to the swallows, when I returned from my Dubrovnik adventure there were five fledglings in the nest, which the parents had economically refurbished from last year. There was one nasty incident when their privacy was invaded by a dear friend with his camera. He took too close a shot of the nestlings and one flew out but managed to struggle back to the rafter beside the nest. The others, finding that they had more room without him, refused to let him back and the member of the paparazzi who had taken the photograph was given a lecture by me on the Invasion of Privacy Bill, which is currently, being debated in the UK.

> *Give me space God so that I can breathe.*
> *Give me love God so that I can live.*

PLEASE RELEASE ME . . . LET ME GO

'IF you believe in life after death, why don't you want to die – especially if you are so convinced that the life after this one will be better?'

My old friend was telling me how he wished to die, and the sooner the better. He was tired, he told me, of this life, and as I have heard this before from several other people, who find the infirmities of age depressing as well as restricting, I was on familiar ground.

Euthanasia is much discussed among the older members of the community. I have sat in on many conversations with people who believe that they have the right to terminate their lives when they feel that there is little point in going on. They usually want to hand the responsibility for the termination over to a doctor, for suicide is for them not an option. These old friends are not on life support machines, with which there are times when medically it is deemed right to switch off the life support. They are people who have lived full lives but find the restrictions and pain of debilitating illness tiresome for them and hard for those who love them to witness.

I happen to believe that however poor the quality of life is, it is still a God-given commodity and not one which can be discarded.

I asked a Buddhist once whether she believed in life after death. She replied that Nirvana – which means 'bliss unspeakable' – has to be striven after in this world and that life after death will depend upon one's progress along that pilgrim way.

Realising that reincarnation is part of that religious belief, I did not pursue the matter. I did not want to think I might come back as some lower life order like a rat!

I feel safer in my own belief. In his poem 'Intimations of Immortality' Wordsworth touched on one aspect of the continuing of life which I like.

> *Though nothing can bring back the hour*
> *Of splendour in the grass, of glory in the flower,*
> *We will grieve not, rather find*
> *Strength in what remains behind . . .*
> *In the human thoughts that spring*
> *Out of human suffering;*
> *In the faith that looks through death,*
> *In the years that bring the philosophic mind.*

THE ADVENT OF THE REAL CHRISTMAS

The Match of the Day Milk Chocolate Calendar contained milk chocolates produced by Bon Bon Buddies. I do not know if it is available this year but last year's calendar was brought to me by a friend as an example of people cashing in on the Christian festival with little idea of what it meant.

The notion of Advent calendars and candles is to mark the days leading up to 25 December and reminding us of the days before

Christmas. I enjoy having both in the house as a prelude to the Christmas celebrations.

Last year's Match of the Day Advent calendar had no religious significance unless, of course, football is your religion. If this is the objective of this particular Advent calendar, it would have been more appropriate if it were leading up to the day when the World Cup was to be played. The countdown could begin 24 days before the final match and presumably the producers could have behind each little window the face of one of the English side plus substitutes, managers, trainers and perhaps heroes from the past.

The organisers of the World Rugby Cup, which has taken up an inordinate amount of my time sitting watching the enormous examples of sheer brute force combining together to form such entertaining rugby on our television screens, might have thought of an Advent Rugby Calendar leading up to the wonderful match at the end of last month.

Advent means quite simply the coming or arrival and the four Sundays preceding the Christian festival of the nativity of Christ are noted as the period of Advent. I have no great objection, as a football enthusiast, to the BBC Match of the Day organisation combining with Bon Bon Buddies producing an advent calendar so long as they do not pretend it is associated in anyway with the coming of Christ.

> Let Christmas not become a thing
> Merely of merchant's trafficking,
> Of tinsel bell and holly wreath
> And surface pleasure but beneath
> The childish glamour let us find
> Nourishment for soul and mind.
> Let us follow kinder ways
> Through our teeming human maze,
> And help the age of peace to come
> From a Dreamer's martyrdom.

Madeline Morse

QUESTIONS OF LIFE AND DEATH

'DO not on any account tell him that it is a geriatric dog's blood test,' Barclay's vet said after he had behaved disgracefully in the surgery. To clarify that, I should perhaps mention that it was Barclay and not the vet who had behaved disgracefully.

'I think you made a rather unnecessary fuss about having a simple blood test,' I said to Barclay, the rather long dog with one ear up and one down, who now shares my life, as we left the surgery. He had struggled and whimpered and made an absolute fool of himself.

I did not mention the word geriatric because Barclay is only seven, going on eight, and I felt somewhat aggrieved to think that he was regarded as a senior citizen while still in the prime of life.

Within three hours his extremely competent and kindly vet telephoned to tell me all was very well indeed.

The next day I received a print-out of the test showing that he had indeed hit the jackpot in all thirteen tests. Cholesterol, albumen and all the other tested functions were perfect.

I have to own that my own experiences of blood tests are of a more prolonged anxiety while waiting for results.

We all worry about medical tests and wait uncomfortably for the results. I get more calls and correspondence from readers of this column about their dread of illness and of dying than on any other subject. I always try to be reassuring and to state categorically that I believe, as a Christian, that death is not the end of our lives, and that we shall in another existence be with God and most probably with those we love after we die.

I am grateful to the person who sent me this poem called Fancy Meeting You.

> I dreamt death came the other night
> And heaven's gates opened wide.
> With kindly grace an angel came
> And ushered me inside.
> And there to my astonishment
> Stood folk I'd known on Earth.
> Some I'd judged as quite unfit
> Or but of little worth.
> Indignant words rose to my lips
> But never were set free,
> For every face showed stunned surprise
> – No one expected me.

BREAKING UP IS HARD TO DO

'BARCLAY? But you're with the Midland,' said the girl at my bank. She had been asking about the name I had given my dog. I told her that his name had been Bruno but he was not at all a macho sort of dog. Dulcie, my depend-upon, had suggested calling him Barclay.

I must own that when he arrived, I thought we should have called him Chips, being an abbreviated form of chipolata. He looked not so much like a sausage dog but like a chipolata on legs. On the certificate which came with him it said he was a dachshund cross. So far I have not worked out which other dog played a part in his breeding. He has the usual markings of a black and tan dog but he is very, very long and very, very thin and determined that I shall not go out of his sight for a single moment. He did content himself with sitting outside the shower, but otherwise he is grafted to me in a quite endearing way.

Poor Barclay was devastated when the young couple who owned him separated. Presumably all that he knew which was familiar and secure disappeared in a flash and he found himself in a shelter awaiting adoption. I had to provide a reference as to my suitability before he could be adopted by me. I have given many references for other people in my time, so this was a new experience – but my vet willingly provided it.

Somehow this little dog's obvious lack of security has caused me to reflect on how dreadful all broken relationships are for those who are damaged by them. No one who has been through a divorce or the break-up of a partnership where children are involved could say that it had been easy for them or for their children.

I have shared with many young couples and with those of mature years who have told me of the anguish which divorce brings. I have listened to children who have never really recovered from the feeling of being abandoned when suddenly the familiar family home is no more.

There is much heard nowadays of the need to make divorce easier. Our own law has changed, and I only hope that it will not mean that those contemplating marriage will see it as a sort of situation in which an easy opt-out clause is built into the commitment.

What is the secret of a good relationship? Goethe wrote something I always remember:

> *Love does not dominate – it cultivates.*

PS: I was intrigued to find that Barclay had hit the national newspaper headlines when he came to live with me – and even more fascinated to read that he had found a home with a wealthy Jersey resident. Pity they did not say rich in friends. It would have been more accurate.

JUDGE PEOPLE BY WHAT THEY ARE

EVERY time I watch the Antiques Road Show I find myself glancing round the sitting room to see if, by any chance, there is lurking a treasure that would make me rich beyond my wildest dreams.

I have already practised what I would say if such a treasure were discovered. I have determined not to follow the usual formula where people whose breath has been taken away by the discovery of the value of Granny's teapot say: 'No, not really. Oh I never guessed!' I have practised a rather nonchalant 'I wondered if it were something like that. Only £40,000 - are you sure?'

Of course the situation will never arise. I had two grandmothers, and if they had teapots or priceless paintings hidden in their attics they are not in my possession. Just as well really, for thieves seem to discover all too quickly houses where there are such treasures.

I have a dear friend who lives in an idyllic setting in the Malvern Hills. She has been twice robbed in the past five years during daylight hours. I mourn some of the lovely things she has lost. I have always known them as part of her home and somehow the spaces where they once stood seem a silent reminder of the avarice in our society.

Sadly, her house has become vulnerable since a motorway was constructed nearby.

Last month I bought a treasure. Well, to be exact it would not fetch a great deal in the open market, but I fell in love with it. It is a little replica of my coal scuttle.

It stands about six inches high, is zinc-lined and the handle and the helmet-shaped cover exactly match Big Brother on the hearth. It was probably made by some apprentice coppersmith as part of his training.

I have polished it once or twice and I hope it will soon resemble my coal scuttle which gleams in the firelight.

> *In God's eyes people are more important than their possessions. So we must never judge them by what they have but by what they are.*

EVEN THE CAMERA CAN LIE

I READ a joke the other day in a book called 'Jokes, Quotes and One-Liners' which a friend gave me.

She said on presenting the book that she felt that there must be times when I needed the odd bit of inspiration. She was quite right, and I found myself leafing through the pages this week when my eye fell on the following anecdote:

Mrs Jones went into a photographer's studio and asked him to enlarge a picture of her late husband. She gave him explicit instructions and concluded by saying: 'And don't forget to take off that awful looking hat.'

The photographer said: 'I think I can do that. What colour hair did he have and what side did he part it on?'

Mrs Jones thought for a moment, then said: 'I can't remember, but when you take off that hat you can see for yourself.'

I don't suppose that the little story would rank highly with those who like sophisticated humour, but I am a simple soul and I chuckled as I went about my chores that day.

Photographers can do extremely clever things with their cameras. They can also fool people with doctored photographs, and I am told that some of the animal films which we see on television owe more to the skill of the editor than to the cleverness of the animal.

I was brought up to believe that the camera cannot lie, and it has taken me a long time to realise the fallacy of that particular statement. The camera lies very well, and fools the gullible very often.

I was looking at some wedding photographs the other day and they were a very professional collection. The mother of the bride and I pored over them, and we both agreed that everyone looked lovely, and I did not have to hurry over the group, of which I formed a part, because even I looked reasonably presentable in a new suit!

We all want to look our best for a photographer. Professional models insist on having their best side photographed, and the rest of us who are not sure which is our best and which our worst side just hope for the best!

Most of us have a good side and a not so good side. The most important think in life is to be true to ourselves and to God, for we can fool neither.

These are the words of Shakespeare:

To thine own self be true.
And it must follow, as the night to any man,
Thou canst not then be false to any man.

PUPPY LOVE

BARCLAY, the very long dog who now shares my life, ought to be a steeplechaser. He can leap over any fence or gate with extraordinary agility, and the fences which were so expensive and adequate for the late Tovey are totally useless for his successor.

Incidentally, I had not realised until I looked up the dictionary reference that a steeplechase was so called because it was originally an impromptu race with some visible church steeple as the goal.

To revert to my steeplechasing dog companion, he leaps the gates and fences to go to visit his friend Penny who lives across the road. She is a five-month-old sheepdog cross puppy and as determined to get into my garden as Barclay is to visit her.

Puppy love is something which is quite endearing and, like calf love, has all the innocence of immaturity. They will play together for hours, and were it not for the fact that even this little road is sometimes used by road hogs with singularly little regard for pedestrians or passionate passing puppies there would not be a problem.

So far I have spent over £50 on extra chickenwire, not to mention the cost of its erection. I did learn an interesting fact about chickenwire which may have been obvious to anyone less dim than me: the smaller the holes the bigger the cost.

We have to have half-inch holes, for anything larger can be widened and allow a very long, thin, determined dog to pass through.

While I was contemplating the last bill of £16.99 for approximately 33 ft by 2 ft of galvanised netting (chickenwire to the cognoscenti), I considered if it would be worth moving to a cottage with a smaller garden. On the other hand, when so much emphasis is placed upon the need for those who find themselves made redundant or reach retirement age to find suitable leisure pursuits, I have had my fence construction as a ready-made hobby.

Barclay does not understand my preoccupation in keeping him safe, and would that I could explain my motives to him.

I wish I had known Martin Elginbrodde, whose epitaph is in the graveyard at Elgin Cathedral. He wanted God to understand his situation, just as I would like Barclay to understand mine.

Here lie I, Martin Elginbrodde;
Have mercy on my soul Lord God,
As I would do were I Lord God
And you were Martin Elginbrodde.

MEMORIES ARE MADE OF THIS

Just a line to say I'm living,
That I'm not among the dead;
Though I'm getting more forgetful,
And more mixed up in the head.
For sometimes I can't remember.
When I stand at the foot of the stair,
If I must go up for something,
Or I've just come down from there.
And before the fridge so often
My poor mind is filled with doubt;
Have I just put food away,
Or have I come to take some out?

THE above lines are part of a poem which a reader sent to me. It ends with this memorable verse:

Here I stand before the mailbox,
With a face so very red,
Instead of mailing you my letter,
I have opened it instead.

We all forget things. Some people have difficulty in remembering names, and others cannot put faces to the names they have remembered. The facts which we put into our memory box early in life we can usually pull out fairly easily. The facts which we post into our memory boxes as we grow older seem to be less easy to recall. It is all part of the ageing process.

People frequently share with me their anxieties about growing old. They do not want to be dependent on other people. They do not want to feel that they are no longer of use. They dread being a burden and spoil the years that are left to them by looking back regretfully. They do not look forward hopefully. I usually try to tell them and myself that there is a time for doing and a time for being.

I have the Nun's Prayer hanging in my bathroom as a reminder to me of some of the truths in that prayer about growing old. On the subject of memory there is a refreshing passage.

I dare not ask for improved memory, but for a growing humility and a lessing cocksuredness when my memory seems to clash with the memories of others. Teach me the glorious lesson that occasionally I may be mistaken!

WAYS AND MEANS TO GET THERE IN THE END

I HAVE never wanted to do anything which could get me into the Guinness Book of Records. It simply would not occur to me to run up Mount Annapurna or slide down Kilimanjaro, and as for walking on my own to the North or South Pole, the very thought makes me shudder.

Some people attempt great feats of endurance in order to be the first to achieve the goal. Others combine their heroic deeds with getting sponsors to raise money for a particular charity.

Thinking along these lines, I found myself considering the case of Sir Ranulph Fiennes, who attempted to walk to the North Pole by himself. He took two sledges for his provisions, which seems fairly reasonable, but apparently he was only able to pull one at a time. So when he had gone so far with the first sledge, he then had to turn back and pull the second one. In this way, he trebled the mileage to the Pole - unless, of course, he had been able to eat his way quickly through the contents of one sledge and then would have been unhampered by having to go back for the other one. I have not read any logistical details of the trip, but it is a mind-boggling thought that this man, who has attempted many hazardous journeys, and returned after hair-raising accounts of frostbite and the like, should have been hell-bent on this new adventure. How sad that it should have failed.

Reverting to the subject of sponsoring people to do tasks of great endurance, I found myself in difficulty last month. A request came to me through the post from Sister Michaela, director of the World Villages for Children. The appeal for help came with a 10p coin and a 2p coin Sellotaped to the letter. She asked me either to return the coins or send a minimum of £10.12 which would help to feed, clothe and educate one child in the children's village. Sister Michaela and her charity are unknown to me.

As I wrote a cheque, I thought it was easier than walking to the North Pole, but I felt slightly blackmailed by this particular form of appeal. After I had posted the envelope I wrote a BB aphorism with which to end this article:

> It is not what we would do if we won a million pounds. It is what we do with the money that we have now.

THE SEVEN MODERN SINS

'YOU can have some Sugar Puffs with milk,' I said to Barclay, the rather long dog who now shares my life, 'I bought them in error and they are too sweet for me.'

Barclay looked anxiously up at me. He has a beguiling look, which is more pronounced because he has one ear up and one ear down. I may have remarked on this characteristic before but I did not wish to make it a feature, lest he achieve either two up or two down, which is a normal ear position as well as a common description of a house.

He just occasionally comes into the kitchen at breakfast to indicate that he is hungry. His one meal a day regime means that his evening supper at five does occasionally leave him feeling peckish in the morning, I suppose.

It was as he was mopping up the last of the Sugar Puffs that I found myself wondering why so much has gone wrong in the world of animal husbandry.

Desperate farmers having suffered the slaughter of their cattle because of BSE are now facing the possibility that their sheep could also be carriers of the disease.

We live in a world where genetic interference with vegetables is now a distinct possibility, and those who have advocated organic production methods no longer seem to be the cranks they once were assumed to be.

I would like to think that Canon Frederic Donaldson was being too cynical when he wrote his version of the seven modern sins. However, when we examine the failures in our modern society, so much could be the result of old sins in modern dress.

Certainly, greed is too often the hallmark of producers of every sort of commodity.

The seven modern sins:

Politics without principles.
Pleasures without conscience.
Wealth without work.
Knowledge without character.
Industry without morality.
Science without humanity.
Worship without sacrifice.

LOOKING FOR THE LORD'S LOVE

I LOST a £20 note on Thursday 17 August. I know roughly where I lost it, but despite retracing my steps I did not find it.

Forty-four years ago I know that losing a £20 note would have been a greater tragedy than this recent loss. Money has, over the years - ever since decimalisation, actually - lost its value.

Twenty pounds 44 years ago when we first moved to Jersey as a family would have been a month's housekeeping allowance. We lived well on just over £4 a week for the basic necessities. That did not include light and heat, but paid the grocer, the butcher, the milkman and the newsagent.

It is true that we were only four in the family, but as I recall, we ate well and I had domestic help for the large manse in which we lived.

I am not the sort of person to let money slip through my fingers, so I was aggrieved by my loss. The fact that I remember the date is an indication that it was burned into my mind that on that day last month when I was a careless idiot. The time I wasted searching was enormous. The steps I retraced were tiring. Looking in the same place over and over again showed how put out I was by this act of stupidity. I even got up in the middle of the night and took the sofa in my bedroom to pieces lest it had dropped down behind the cushions.

Eventually, I accepted the fact that I was not going to find it and, furthermore, realised that I must not lose any more sleep over it.

I know those who patiently read this column week by week will empathise with me. Have we not all at some time lost something? The house key, the car ignition key seem to have a curious way of hiding just when they are most needed.

I lost a golf club once when I put it down on the course and chose another club from the bag and left the original one lying there. I learned from the golf club professional that many lost clubs were brought to him, but mine never appeared.

Thinking of things I have lost, I wrote this little prayer for careless people like me:

Lord let us never lose heart or patience. Help us always to remember that nothing is more precious than Your love which we can never lose.

A HELPING HAND WHERE IT'S NEEDED

I AM not a catalogue freak, but I could be one. I have friends who scarcely ever enter a shop but depend on catalogues to supply their needs. They leaf through the shiny pages of tempting goods and send off for clothes or furnishings and all manner of goodies. When the items come, they try them on or try them out and mention casually when a friend admires a new acquisition that they got it by post.

I have never had one of these thick books which people who belong to Christmas clubs favour.

The principle is quite simple for one pays so much a week and then the organiser comes round and shows the catalogue to a subscriber and takes the order.

Other shoppers by post rely on magazine or newspaper advertisements which illustrate garments or goods and by filling in a coupon and sending a cheque or mentioning one's plastic card number the goods are dispatched by return.

I have occasionally been presented with a garment by such a shopper who discovers that the reality did not match the description and finding that it fitted and suited a friend or neighbour passed the parcel!

Recently, I borrowed a Master Catalogue from an occupational therapist who works with those who need specially adapted gadgets to make life easier. The catalogue was full of most imaginatively designed household and other pieces of equipment and I pored over it for hours. My own favourite kitchen bottle and jar opener was illustrated and, as I noted in the Arthritis Research magazine that a reader had had difficulty in finding such a gadget, I was glad that they are still obtainable. It is simply a plastic cone-shaped cup with a rubber lining which fits on to a wall. Mine has for years been inside the kitchen cupboard. With one hand I can open screw-top bottles and jars with no difficulty.

Someone gave me the device when I broke my wrist and I would never want to be without it. I am going to order another one or two through my occupational therapist acquaintance lest mine breaks or someone else needs one.

For the permanently disabled life can be very hard, and it is good that there are those whose vocation is to help to make life easier for them. Here is a prayer for those who help with their skill and those who need such professional help.

> *Give me patience to help those who need my skill and give those who are dependent on others' patience to live with their problems and pain.*

COMFORT IN THE SLEEP OF THE BLESSED

'I HAVE a poem by John Marston here on my brass clip about a dog called Delight,' I said to Barclay, the rather long dog with one ear up and one ear down, who was lying on his bed in the Granary.

Those who have read this column for a long time will know that my study is called the Granary after my mother of blessed memory, who was known as Gran.

Barclay was not in the mood for talk, for he had just come in after chasing round Penny's garden. Penny is his girlfriend who lives in the house opposite ours across the little road in our valley.

'I shall read it to you as I put it on the word processor, I said. Barclay did not even open an eye.

> I was a scholar.
> The more I learnt, the more I learnt to doubt.
> Delight, my spaniel, slept
> Whilst I wasted lamp oil,
> And still my spaniel slept.
>
> I thought, quoted, read, observed
> And prayed,
> Read many books,
> And still my spaniel slept.
>
> At length he waked and yawned
> And by yon sky
> For ought I know
> He knew as much as I.

As I finished reading and getting the poem on my machine ready for printing, Barclay yawned, opened his eyes and looked at me. Delight and he had much in common, and I suppose the writer of the poem and I enjoyed similar pursuits: reading, praying, observing and living with a dog as companion.

I enjoy my life and I think Barclay enjoys his, and at the end of the day we know how blessed we are.

> God, make me content with my lot, grateful to You for being
> there when I need You, and friends to brighten my way.

LOOKING AFTER THE SANDS OF TIME

'MUMMY, in heaven will the tide always be in?' was a question asked years ago by a four-year-old who was faced with the West Park beach on a day when the tide was at its lowest.

Contemplating the walk to the sea was rather more than her four-year-old legs could manage, and her question has always lingered at the back of my mind.

I am not an expert on the effects on the beaches of tidal changes. I have noted over the years that some of the beaches which used to be great sandy areas where children could dig and bury their parents in the sand seem to have changed their character.

We are, however, not alone in this. An article in my national paper recently about the mile-long curving beach of Swanage, once so beloved by families who enjoyed a proper seaside holiday, highlighted the disappearance of sand from that once famous beach. The local council blames the weather, the tides and global warming for the changing face of Swanage beach.

However, one resident who rents beach concessions from the council blames the 60-yard stone jetty in the middle of the bay. This recently built jetty apparently carries away storm water which, in the past, has caused dangerous flooding in the area. However, land reclamation and man-made jetties are not the only threat to beaches, according to one expert. Beaches have a finite life now that global warming is raising sea levels.

We live in a strange world where that which we emit from our household appliances and factories causes problems to our environment. Unless we can control our emissions it would appear that we will lose more of our planet to the sea.

Reverting to my little friend - now herself the mother of children - who wanted to know about heavenly beaches, I am afraid I am not an authority on such matters.

However, I do know that although we may try to ruin this earth, we have an obligation to be good tenants while always being mindful of the heavenly state which Christ promised us.

> *The quietness of that threshold of heaven . . . is always there for us like an old church porch in a street where the traffic thunders by, if only we can manage to forget ourselves and our busyness for long enough to become conscious of it, to get out of the traffic and go in.*

St Francis of Assisi

WHEN YOUR BACK IS TO THE WALL

'DOCTORS' hearts sink when confronted by a patient complaining of backache (*Doctor Thomas Stuttaford writes*). The causes are legion and the best that can be said is that a cure can never be guaranteed. The pain may well stem from long-standing injuries, often minor but repetitive ones which can later be complicated by secondary arthritis, in which spikes of bone may touch a nerve, causing acute pain.'

I read that passage in an article regarding the Prince of Wales, whose backache has caused him problems of late, and the announcement that he had had to cancel his engagements will generate a wave of sympathy from everyone who has ever suffered the agonies of the damned which severe back pain can cause.

I have friends who are 'martyrs to their backs'. They bowl along quite happily for weeks, months or years and then suddenly they are reminded of their weakness by either an agonising pain or a dull ache. Both are the forerunner of the devil which lurks in the vertebrae.

The devil who is resident in vertebrae has an odd sense of humour. I can recall standing at the telephone some years ago fixing a game of golf for a couple of hours later. As I turned away from the telephone I felt a searing pain and it took me some moments to re-dial the friend's number and state that I would not after all be able to play.

I will not bore my readers with the explanation which I proffered to my unbelieving golfing chum. Nor will I dwell upon the crawl to my bedroom, where I lay on the floor cursing the devil who had, as devils always do, attacked me when my back was turned!

Since that time I have had very infrequent battles with the Back Devil. In the light of these very minor experiences, I can sympathise and emphasise with Prince Charles. I know the pain and everyone who has suffered as he has will feel for him.

It is a fact of life that it is not until we have suffered a similar illness, misfortune or loss that we can fully share in the suffering of someone else. Of course, we can try to imagine the agony of someone who has endured a fearful tragedy. However, most of the time we are not called upon to stand by those who have suffered some ghastly misfortune.

Most of the blows life deals are common at some stage in life to all of us. We react differently, but it is comforting to know that a friend is on hand who may, perhaps, be able to share some of the anguish because they too have felt a similar pain.

You may be sorry that you spoke, sorry you stayed or went,
sorry you won or lost, sorry so much was spent. But, as you
go through life you'll find you're never sorry you were kind.

MORNING LARKS AND NIGHT OWLS

IT is a strange thing that people with opposite temperaments seem quite often to marry each other or, in these days, choose to live together.

I do not know whether a sociologist has ever studied why it is that people with lark-like tendencies who leap out of bed in the morning bright-eyed and bushy-tailed are partnered by those owl-like creatures who stay up half the night and for whom waking up in the morning presents a daily challenge.

I am in the lark category. Morning cannot come too soon for me, and I need no cups of tea to get me out of bed. I was, however, married to a man who was unable to wake up until he had drunk at least two cups of strong tea.

He bought, over the years, several automatic tea-making devices. They all required a certain amount of input from him, mostly in the shape of putting water in the little kettle the night before and two teabags in the teapot which was positioned alongside the kettle. Alas, there were human errors. Boiling water pouring out of the little kettle on to the bedside table was a commonplace malfunction. The teapot had not been put in position. On other occasions the teabags were forgotten and there were anguished groans as mouthfuls of hot water were gulped down by my half-asleep husband.

Because we are all so different and stress can result in relationships in the home and in the work place, we should remember Dr Barclay's morning prayer:

> O God our Father help us through this day so to live that we
> may bring help to others, credit to ourselves and to the name
> we bear, and joy to those who love us and to you.
> Cheerful when things go wrong;
> Persevering when things are difficult;
> Serene when things are irritating.
> Enable us to be:
> Helpful to those in difficulties;
> Kind to those in need;
> Sympathetic to those whose hearts are sore and sad.
> Grant that:
> Nothing may make us lose our tempers;
> Nothing may take away our joy;
> Nothing may ruffle our peace;
> Nothing may make us bitter towards anyone.
> So grant us through all this day all with whom we work, and
> all those whom we meet, may see in us the reflection of the
> Master, whose we are and whom we seek to serve. This we
> ask for your love's sake.

A SMALL DOSE OF DANGER

'YOU'D better have a dose of your medicine,' I said to Barclay, the rather long dog with one ear up and one down who now shares my life. He was sitting staring mournfully at one of his favourite dog biscuits, so I knew that he was suffering from his dicky tummy syndrome, which usually leads to up-chuck.

Barclay and I are both martyrs to up-chuck, which is the American name for those of us who have difficulty at times in keeping food down. I have had an uneasy hiatus hernia for years and Barclay has got a rather delicate digestive system and what he asks his stomach to digest is more than it can bear at times.

I am allergic to shellfish and he, strangely enough, is allergic to chicken and all poultry. His allergy to poultry is hard because roast chicken on Sunday for dinner does smell delicious and he sits in the kitchen licking his lips as the savoury smell drifts towards him.

My allergy to shellfish goes back a very long way to a lobster dinner eaten in wartime London. It was a romantic meal by candlelight and until that moment the love affair, which was at the stage of the romance of the first date, was progressing well. I will draw a veil over the agony that followed the lobster dinner. It was not an evening I care to remember and believing it must have been a rather elderly lobster, I determined to try the delicious shellfish on another occasion.

This time the lobster was newly caught and was wandering about in the boot of my car. Driving up from the little fishing village of Newtonhill, south of Aberdeen, I contemplated the meal ahead. Alas, the London experience was repeated and the doctor who was called told me that I must never eat shellfish again.

Barclay and I share the same bottle of Milk of Magnesia. His plastic spoon is attached to the bottle with an elastic band; I get mine from the cutlery drawer.

The other evening with a violent attack of indigestion I rushed to the kitchen cupboard, grabbed the bottle, poured out a dose and before I realised it I had used his spoon! It did not do me any harm, but I felt even more squeamish for a little while.

Thinking of spoons, I remembered an old Scottish saying, which is a warning about flirting with danger:

When ye sup with the devil ye need a long spoon.

A FLIGHT OF FANCY IN THE SMALL HOURS

IT was half past two in the morning. Outside it was dark and in the stillness of the late September night I was conscious that Bennie, my holiday companion, and I were not alone in the delightful Brittany farmhouse which kind friends lend us each year for a holiday. There seemed to be movements in the corridor outside my bedroom and I lay fearful under the duvet.

Suddenly there was an appalling noise downstairs - shrieks as if murder were afoot, and the sound of rattling glass as though the contestants in some fracas were chasing each other round the house.

We had two choices: to pull our duvets over our heads and pray for morning, or venture downstairs to see what was happening.

I have never believed that pulling a duvet over the head will make trouble disappear. There was also a vague sense of responsibility to our dear friends whose house, at that moment, appeared to be the centre of some sort of major attack.

Donning slippers and dressing gowns and with our hearts uncomfortably in our respective mouths, we slowly crept down stairs.

As we reached the last step I switched on the light. At that moment an owl flew past us, hotly pursued by another one. Silently we crossed the room, avoiding some of the evidence of their nervous reaction to chasing each other down the chimney, and opened the windows and doors. One owl thankfully escaped but the other was of a more sociable turn of mind. He preceded us upstairs, flew into one of the unoccupied bedrooms, perched on the curtain rail and went to sleep.

We opened the window, bade him good night and after cleaning up the granite tiles in the kitchen and hall went back to bed confident that he would awake and go home.

However, he decided not only to have a sleepover with us, but stayed for the whole of the next day, despite our pleadings. By dusk we thought he ought to be encouraged to seek the wide open spaces.

Paul, who can cope with every situation and who lives next door, came wearing thick gloves and gently told the bird to hop off the curtain rail and go back to his owl friends. Reluctantly he left, but not before I stroked his tail feathers, to which he submitted graciously.

Thinking of our initial fear when the owls woke us up, I remembered the old Cornish prayer:

> *From ghoulies and ghosties and long-legged beasties*
> *And things that go bump in the night,*
> *Good Lord deliver us.*

SHINING THROUGH A WINDOW OF OPPORTUNITY

ON reflection, I should not perhaps have tried the electric bed which was on sale in a well known furniture shop in Bath Street.

Obviously, before buying a new bed it is wise to try it out. The mattress may be too soft or too hard, so lying on a bed is not an unreasonable thing to do before spending a good deal of money on the purchase.

I am, it has to be owned, not an authority on buying new beds. My present bed came with Mother when she moved down from Scotland to make her home in Jersey. When she left me physically to be with others whom I have loved and lost for a while, I moved her bed down to my room. I got rid of my old bed and rebedded the spare room.

I did not buy new beds for replacements, but got second-hand ones which were advertised in this paper. When my friends remonstrated with me over buying second-hand beds, stating that they would be fearful sleeping in such beds, I was amazed. Had they not slept in hotel beds all over the world? Thousands of people had slept in those beds, people whom they did not know, whereas I knew the owners of my second-hand beds and the homes from which my beds had come.

However, the time had come for me to splash out - not on a water bed, but on an electric bed - and that is how I found myself lying in the shop window in Bath Street while the most helpful assistant pressed a button and I suddenly sat up.

Passers-by, one or two who recognised me, found the sight diverting. A small crowd gathered and I suggested to the one who held the remote control that she should up-end the bottom half of the bed to show its versatility. This denied the onlookers the sight of my prostrate form in its entirety.

I should have taken a curtain call when I left the window, but by then I was finding my overexposure somewhat embarrassing and I withdrew.

I have not bought a bed yet. Others have yet to be tried, I hope in the comparative privacy of the showroom.

I found a quotation the other days which applies to the Christian life - and to windows.

> *If a window of opportunity opens, do not pull down the shade.*

SHARING FEARS GIVES COURAGE TO CARRY ON

BARCLAY, the rather long dog with one ear up and one ear down, did not really expect to be taking the salute with the Bailiff on Saturday at the Foire de Jèrri Country Show 2000. It is not the sort of thing that I could have explained to him in advance had I known this singular honour was about to befall him.

We went to the Foire to sell and sign his book 'A Sheltered Life' and I was asked if I would go on the dais while the performance took place. As Barclay and I are joined not exactly like Siamiese twins at the hip, but certainly at the heart and by his lead, he had no option but to come with me.

We watched the Royal Horse Artillery giving their absolutely flawless and totally remarkable performance.

The marching band came almost right up to the dais and Barclay was transfixed at the sight and sound of such magnificence.

When the Bailiff got up to take the salute we stood up and those of us on two legs and the one on four legs behaved with great dignity.

I worried a little about the Royal Horse Artillery when they came quite near to us at full gallop, but by then, what with the heat and the excitement, Barclay was having a little sleep.

When the cannon fired he opened one eye and then dropped off again. He is neither gun-shy nor fireworks-wary. Penny-over-the-road, his sheepdog friend, was frightened two years ago by the cannon at the Howard Davis show and she has never regained her confidence about loud noises, Fireworks are an absolute nightmare to her as, indeed, they are to many dogs.

Fear, whether it is rational or irrational, is a burden with which animals and we human beings have to cope. Phobias - that is, irrational fears - like my phobia about mice, cannot always be treated, but people who suffer from more ordinary fears which have a basis in reality can usually be helped.

It is by facing our fears and sharing them with God, who is the power within us, that we find courage to go on.

BEWARE OF INANIMATE OBJECTS

'DON'T lift it by the arms. It loves it when people do that. It can trap your whole hand in its powerful grip,' I shouted as a friend tried to move one of the garden chairs.

Articles in magazines and newspapers about garden furniture never mention the dangers which lurk in the most innocent-looking outdoor chair or table.

It all began with the forerunners of modern garden furniture when we, who were not born yesterday, were wont to have our fingers crushed by deckchairs with striped canvas seats. If they did not crush our fingers in a fit of pique, they would stretch out and deposit us on the wet grass, causing back problems for the rest of our lives. These chairs, were not, as we would say today, 'user friendly'.

We had one particularly malevolent chair in my family home which always looked as if it were correctly erected and would then slip off its slotted strut at the rear and collapse in a heap. Occasionally it caught the fingers of the unwary as well as doing spinal damage as it folded up.

As the years passed and garden furniture design improved, I bought some upright director-style canvas chairs with swivel backs. They dislike children and could project a small child through the back with a quick flick of swinging canvas.

At the same time I had a garden table which seemed able to fold two of its four legs with disastrous results to the garden china.

Some of my present garden furniture is made of rigid indestructible plastic. Long after I am dead I am sure that archaeologists will dig up pieces of white plastic and try to piece together the life of the inhabitants of the area who lived some 500 years before their excavation. Little will they know that the piece of plastic, when it was a garden chair, would fold up at will and trap the unwary who grasped it by its arms.

I have learned to treat all garden furniture with deep suspicion and a healthy respect. Items seem, like many inanimate objects, to have mind of their own.

The chair on which I am sitting in front of my word processor as I write this article always sighs when I sit down on it. It is a work-shy chair, of that I have no doubt at all.

> *Dear God, may the things which I possess never possess*
> *me. Let me always remember that only truth, tolerance and*
> *compassion and other gifts of the spirit are everlasting.*

IF YOU ARE THERE, GOD

I DO not know how many people pray during the course of their daily lives.

Some make a habit of this at night or in the morning. Others tell me they pray at the kitchen sink or sometimes in the office while waiting for a client.

Others assure me that when they are fishing and waiting for a fish to bite in the quietness of the reservoir, or in the boat waiting for the mackerel to take the bait, they frequently say the odd prayer - and not just for a fish to rise. In the silence they find they can talk to God about a problem which is overshadowing their lives at the time.

People nearly all pray at times of emergency. 'If you are there, God, for Pete's sake help me' is a quite common invocation.

Nervous travellers usually murmur a prayer as the plane takes off or lands, and I am sure that all round the airports of the world the air must be positively hallowed with the prayers of those who wonder if the pilot, to whom they have entrusted their lives, is really competent.

The best known prayer is the Lord's Prayer - and unlike most of our prayers it is a corporate prayer. In our personal prayers we may well say, 'O God, for Pete's sake help me', but in the Lord's Prayer there is no 'I'. It is a prayer which we say with others for others.

A neighbour lent me this poem, which is a reminder of this fact. It is entitled 'Thoughts On The Lord's Prayer', and it is by Charles Thompson.

> *You cannot pray the Lord's Prayer,*
> *And even once say 'I'.*
> *You cannot pray the Lord's Prayer,*
> *And even once say 'my'.*
> *You cannot pray the Lord's Prayer,*
> *And not pray for another;*
> *For when you ask for Daily Bread,*
> *You must include your brother.*
> *For others are included,*
> *In each and every plea;*
> *From the beginning to the end of it,*
> *It does not once say 'me'.*

GOOD ADVICE CAN BE A REAL EYE-OPENER

'TRY cold tea,' suggested the dog expert at the other end of the telephone.

I had rung to ask if she had in her establishment anything for a runny eye. Her establishment caters for all dogs' beauty needs and preparations, as well as food and potions for many creatures who share God's Kingdom. I had consulted her because Barclay, the rather long dog who now shares my life, had got a watery eye. It did not seem bad enough for a vet's appointment, so I had rung my other animal adviser.

'You simply get a teabag and when it's cold squeeze it gently into the eye. If it doesn't improve, go to the vet,' she said.

I thanked her and, in no time at all, Barclay was seated on a kitchen chair and I had a cold teabag in my hand. The instruction had seemed so simple. I squeezed the teabag but my consultant's teabags must be made of sterner stuff because the paper broke and Barclay was understandably aggrieved to find his eye full of tealeaves.

I do not have an eye dropper, so I got a tiny jug and poured some cold tea into that and waited until Barclay's confidence was restored and tried again. This time I achieved the desired result, although I have to own that having to face even a tiny jug poised over his eye did not do a great deal for Barclay's morale, but I applied the treatment twice and the next day his eye was better.

It is such a privilege to help others, and when I asked for advice I was grateful that my dog-loving friend took time in a busy day to give it.

God gives us advice when we ask for it. This short passage by an unknown writer has nothing to do with teabags and dogs, but it has something to do with our responsibility for helping others.

Why?
On the street I saw a small girl cold and shivering in a
thin dress with little hope of a decent meal. I became angry
and said to God: 'Why did you permit this? Why don't
you do something about it?' For a while God said nothing.
That night he replied, quite suddenly: 'I certainly did
something about it. I made you.'

FONTS OF ALL WISDOM

I ENJOYED Kate's christening. I enjoyed it particularly because there were so many children present and they, like their mothers, had dressed up for the occasion.

I had forgotten to wear a big hat, which is almost an obligatory part of wedding and christening outfits, but there were some very elegant pieces of millinery among the congregation.

The small boys were especially nattily dressed. Tom, Kate's brother, wore a double-breasted striped jacket with plain trousers, and some of his friends favoured a matching jacket and trouser effect which set off their three-, four- and five-year-old figures very well.

The small girls were not to be outdone in the fashion contest, and some of them looked as if they had stepped straight out of the pages of a junior Vogue magazine.

Lest readers might begin to think that there were no fathers and other male guests present, I have to admit that they looked as if they had on their city clothes, and in no way let down their wives and children.

Everyone behaved well at the church service. The godparents went through their responses as if to the manner born, and the Rector did not drop Kate – which was just as well.

I always feel just a little sentimental at baptismal services, because it seems to me that generations of parents have stood around the fonts of churches throughout Christendom and prayed that their children shall be brought up in the faith. Not all fulfil the vows made on their behalf, but at the service the intention is to do one's best to bring up a child in the knowledge of God's love.

I shall end with a rather less serious story which I heard recently. It concerned a rather elderly canon who fell asleep during morning service. The curate, realising it was time for the canon to lead the congregation in the recital of the Creed, bent over his sleeping superior and murmured gently: 'I believe in God.'

The canon woke with a start and said: 'So do I, my boy.'

A belief in God is the first step on the road to certainty.

WITHERING OF THE PALM LEAVES

MOST people want to be liked. It is an unusual person who sets out determined to be disliked.

Some people may protest when questioned and say categorically: 'I don't care if people like me or not.' That is usually said defiantly, and one can sense behind the words a determination to make a stand.

But the majority of people, if questioned under oath, would express a desire to be not only liked but popular.

The desire for popularity begins at a very early age, when we attend our first school.

Children can be exceedingly cruel to each other and many well-balanced adults will speak of their early schooldays when they felt outside the chosen circle. Some leader would lord it over the others, and those on the fringe would get their first taste perhaps of feeling unwanted.

It is a tiny step from the feeling of being unwanted to trying to buy popularity in some way or another.

Clever children start up rival gangs, and this is a sensible step. If you cannot get into the magic circle, you start your own circle - and these circles become the nucleus of gangs.

As these youngsters grow up they become members of clubs and societies. I can recall in my early schooldays being the leader of a secret society which was so confidential that no one knew the rules at all. I know that one had to produce an eight of diamonds card to be a member, and I suspect that there were puzzled parents trying to find missing eights of diamonds when playing bridge during the reign of the mysterious Eight of Diamonds Secret Society.

To be accepted and to be one of the gang is something which remains with us as we grow older. To be out on a limb by oneself is a lonely business, and most people prefer the safety of the sheep fold to the wilderness experience.

On Palm Sunday we see how quickly popularity can turn to rejection in the life of Christ. One day he was being heralded as the King, and palm leaves marked his ceremonial procession. In no time at all the crowds who cried hosanna were shouting crucify, and his brief popularity was over.

At the end of the day it is not what other people think of us
. . . it is what God thinks of us.

IT CAN BE HARD TO REJECT THE SOFT OPTION

'WE'LL be able to buy it at the Co-op. We could make a point of getting it on double-divie days,' my friend Bob said. 'I mean, just imagine cannabis, ecstasy, and heroin will all be available on the shelves!'

We had been discussing the drug conference which took place last month in the Island. Delegates from all over the world had come to discuss the best way of tackling the problems which are facing their relevant governments.

I did not go to any of the conference sessions, largely because I am not open-minded about the drug culture. Indeed, I would go so far as to say that I would actively campaign against any suggestion that drugs should be decriminalised and my friend Bob, who holds similar views to mine, was bemoaning the fact that there were those who advocated legalising them because policing pushers and their customers was very difficult.

Most people suggest that cannabis being a so-called soft drug could easily be made available. I would not object to it being prescribed by doctors to those with the medical condition of multiple sclerosis, who appear to be helped by it. I have a friend who is a young wife and mother of two children who suffers from MS. If it were proved clinically to be a help to her and to others with her illness I would certainly not object. However, I do regret those who advocate its use as a recreational drug believing, as I do, that the so-called soft drugs can, and often do lead to hard drug addiction.

Leafing through a book entitled 'Meditations for Women' I found this sentence: 'One of the effects of the addictive process is that we gradually lose contact with our personal morality and we slowly deteriorate as a moral person.'

That sums up very clearly the gradual deterioration which takes place in those who use any form of drugs, whether it be alcohol or cannabis, as an aid to tackling life's problems or because they believe they are a harmless pleasure. They do not solve problems nor are they harmless.

Saying no may be hard, saying yes may be disastrous.

THE GOSPEL ACCORDING TO YOU

I AM not able to eat chocolate or shellfish. I am allergic to both and my life is poorer because of it.

I used to love lobsters and can still recall going down the Scottish coast to Newtonhill, where a willing fisherman would sell me a huge newly caught lobster. I did not in those days agonise about killing fish or animals and having no shellfish allergy I could enjoy the lobster hugely

Nowadays I am more squeamish and had to give up fishing because of my inability to kill a trout or a salmon having landed one of them after an exciting time playing the fish on the end of the line.

I read recently that there is now a theory that the fish do suffer pain and fear when they are hooked and that makes me feel even more guilty about the pleasurable hours on the loch or on the riverside.

It would be good if I could report that I am now a vegetarian but, alas, I am such a hypocrite that I allow others to kill the meat and the fish for my pleasure.

My allergy to crustaceans prevents me enjoying the moules, crabs and lobsters which are such delicious delights on the Island menu but I enjoy fish and meat.

On the question of chocolate, I smiled when I read that Nestlé, that great provider of delicious chocolate, has decided that, from the beginning of this month, Rolos will no longer be advertised as the sort of love gifts which are offered by a suitor. The image has become old-fashioned and Rolos are to become much more sex symbols, as the manufacturers of the chocolates feel relationships have changed and buyers will be attracted by the sexier suggestions.

Goodness me, I thought as I read about the new policy There is not really anything very sexy about a packet of Rolos but it will be interesting to watch the campaign dispassionately.

When one thinks of the agony which advertisers must go through to think up new campaigns to persuade us to sample their wares I wonder how they rate their success - presumably by increased sales of their products.

I came across a yellowed piece of paper in one of my books the other day. It really shows how those who have faith should advertise their product.

> *You're writing a gospel a chapter a day.*
> *By the things that you do*
> *And the words that you say.*
> *Men read what you write,*
> *Be it faithless or true,*
> *Pray what is the gospel*
> *According to you?*

LIVING SIDE BY SIDE BY GEORGE

'ALL the men in this village are called George,' announced the Croatian guide who was escorting us on the coach tour of the lower mountain region north of Dubrovnik.

At that moment, three small boys aged about seven years old ran over to survey the tourists who had been decanted from the bus. 'Have they all been christened George?' I asked. The guide confirmed that this was so.

Stravea was the name of the small village and one can only imagine how, if one shouted George at the top of one's voice, old men, young men and boys would all appear to answer the call.

I rather lost the plot when it came to discovering exactly why this extraordinary state of affairs existed. It may have been to do with St George, the dragon slayer who certainly seemed to have been very active in this part of Croatia. There were churches named after him, paintings depicting the dragon lying in extremis at his feet and quite a number of statues showing the brave George with one foot on the dying dragon and the other holding up either a flag or a sword.

Having grown accustomed to the idea that he was an English saint, it was strange to find him so prominent in the country that was, not so long ago known, Yugoslavia and prior to that had been part of the Austrian empire.

There has, of course, been much discussion recently about George's suitability as England's patron saint and there has been a suggestion that perhaps Alban, that early missionary, might be a better choice.

George was a most popular saint – except, I imagine, with dragons - for Russia, Sweden and England, to name but a few countries, have all claimed him as their patron.

To revert to the village of Georges, it must really be very inconvenient to have all one's menfolk bearing the same name. Introductions would be very difficult, for having a father called George, all one's brothers named George as well as having Uncle George and Grandfather George would make for difficulties. Having every husband christened George is positively mind-boggling.

While on the subject of christening, I love to see the babies brought to the font and hear the young parents making their vows. There is a verse in a baptismal hymn written by Derek Farrow which emphasises this.

> *These joyful parents strengthen, Lord,*
> *And help them to provide*
> *A Christian home, where faithfulness*
> *And patient love abide.*

THE PEOPLE UNDER THE CLOTHES

ABOUT a month ago there was some correspondence in The Times about the contrast in the standards of dress between men and women. The general tone of the letters to the editor seemed to indicate that the female of the species, whether young or old, was better dressed than the male members of society.

One distinguished naval officer, a vice-admiral, no less, was highly critical of men sporting 'hairy legs, too tight shorts, beer bellies, navel-level open-neck shirts, dirty jeans and half-shaved faces escorting mostly very well-dressed females'.

Other letter writers drew attention to the falling standards of dress of opera and concert-goers.

Yet another writer wished that lady members of orchestras would wear full-length black evening dresses with sleeves cut 'More for ease of execution than for style'. I think execution in that sense referred to musical ability and not in preparation for having one's head chopped off.

The only time I found myself surprised in a London theatre was not so much by what members of the audience were wearing but by the unexpected behaviour of a family seated in front of me in the stalls. The mother of the party produced from a capacious shopping bag a sliced loaf and a margarine carton. She then proceeded to make sandwiches for her party of four with some paté, which smelled delicious!

Brought up in the era of little tea trays slid discreetly by a member of the theatre staff to those who had had the foresight to order interval refreshment, I found the stalls picnic a novel experience.

How we behave and how we dress are merely outward indications of what sort of people we are. We all have prejudices because of our backgrounds and training. I myself do not like what is called nowadays designer stubble. To me it looks like a man who has forgotten to shave but I understand from some of my young friends that it is very cool.

At the end of the day, it is not what we wear but most importantly the sort of people we are that matters.

While on the subject of how we relate to people this is an interesting thought:

> *People have discovered that they can fool the Devil, but they can't fool the neighbours.*

E W Howe

RED TED AND A TUG OF LOVE

'I'M not sure that he can take another operation,' I said gloomily to Barclay, the rather long dog who shares my life.

Barclay blinked as if he were choking back an imaginary tear. I looked at him for a moment or two and then glanced at the patient who was sitting on the kitchen table.

Red Ted, so named because he is a red teddy bear, was given to Barclay some months ago and although he appears to be devoted to his companion, his treatment of him is far from gentle. If ever there was a battered-bear syndrome, Red Ted would be a perfect example.

133

After the last assault his right leg was almost totally severed. On that occasion I had to take him to the kitchen theatre and stitch it on, taking care to stuff his innards back at the same time.

Needlework was my worst subject at school, and there has scarcely been a improvement since those far-off days, so my ministrations to Red Ted have not been of the sort that would have received any plaudits from the top brass at the Royal School of Needlework. However, I realised that while my stitches in time do not normally save nine, they might, on this occasion, give Red Ted another week or two of life.

I got out the sewing case and threaded a needle with matching red cotton and sewed Red Ted's left leg back on to his body. This leg was slightly thinner because some of his stuffing had blown away, but the end result was quite good.

An hour later I looked out of the window and saw that Penny, Barclay's sheepdog friend and neighbour, had got one of Red Ted's ears and Barclay had the other one and a tug-of-love was taking place. I use the description tug-of-love carefully for, unlike a tug-of-war where there is always a finish when one side pulls the other over the mark in the middle of the contest, in a tug-of-love contest there is never a finish.

The battles rage and the innocents trapped in the middle have to try to grow up between warring parents.

Alas, one cannot mend broken hearts with a needle and thread. All we can do is to apply patches of love when possible.

> *Be with those who have lost faith in love, and comfort with*
> *Your presence their broken lives.*

PEACE WITHIN WITH HELP FROM WITHOUT

'MY diary's not waterproof so I'll have to call you back,' I said as I replaced the telephone carefully on the little stool beside the bath.

I bath only twice a week, so these sessions are apt to be more prolonged than the showers which I enjoy on the other five days.

I always take the telephone into the bathroom during these times when I lie thinking about he day ahead and occasionally praying about anything which is troubling me. I know kneeling is the conventional attitude of prayer, but as far as I am concerned, I pray whenever I am alone and the bath is as good as the little *prie-dieu* in my bedroom.

Certainly that little antique chair requires me to kneel on it, but anyone can talk to God standing at the sink washing the dishes, or sitting at the computer waiting for inspiration.

People often ask me how to pray, and I suggest that whenever they are alone they stop and talk to God or, if they do not believe in God, they talk to the power outside themselves and share their joys and sorrows. At the end of the day what we all want is inner peace and the knowledge that someone listens and cares.

Someone sent me this personal description of prayer a little while ago. The language suggests that it was written in the days when 'brawn' was a familiar word meaning physical strength and not that old culinary dish consisting of a pig or calf's head cooked and pressed into a pot. I would be happy to pray for physical strength, but potted head, so beloved by some, has never been something I could swallow!

> *I asked for strength and God gave me difficulties to make*
> *me strong.*
> *I asked for wisdom and God gave me brawn to work,*
> *I asked for courage and God gave me danger to overcome,*
> *I asked for love and God gave me troubled people to help,*
> *I asked for favours and God gave me opportunities,*
> *I received nothing I wanted; instead received everything I*
> *needed.*

THE DAY MY POT LUCK RAN OUT

I AM sure that I have written before in Saturday Special that I am not inclined to make New Year resolutions. Experience has taught me that it is not too difficult to make resolutions – the difficulty is keeping them.

However, this year an unfortunate incident in this very month has made me resolve not to put a chicken carcass in a pan of water with the intention of making stock and then going into town leaving the water boiling.

I was in St Helier and gazing at a chicken in a butcher's stall in the market when I remembered the chicken carcass. I stood stock still (forgive the unintended pun, dear readers) and then did a rapid walk back to the car. Of course, I did not ask the Almighty to turn the electricity down under the pan, but I did utter a prayer of hopefulness that the water had not entirely boiled away. Alas, as soon as I opened the door into the cottage I realised that it had!

Smoke greeted me as I raced through the Granary, the dining-room and the sitting-room to reach the kitchen. I found that there was nothing left of the chicken carcass, and the pan, which had been the largest of the copper-bottomed set, was reduced to a blackened mess. The kitchen was full of acrid smoke, and despite flinging doors and windows open, the smell was absolutely dreadful.

I have had to have the walls of the kitchen washed down and all the paintwork renewed. I am still trying to get the ceramic top of the cooker clean. My insurance company and the assessor were very understanding, and John, the painter, has done a fine job.

I then left for a pre-arranged 12-day London break and came back to find everything gleaming - but I have to own that the smell still lingers on after nearly three weeks. At the moment of writing, an aromatic candle is burning lily-of-the valley oil in the sitting room and an electric device is burning oil of freesias in the kitchen.

The making of the chicken soup has caused me some discomfort, and there have certainly been problems to solve.

In a book called 'Positive Thoughts' and sub-titled 'Living Your Life to the Fullest', someone called M Scott Peck wrote this. I hope it is true.

> *It is only because of problems that we grow mentally and spiritually.*

HELP FOR THOSE WHO WILL NOT SEE

'MY hair is grey,' the three-year-old little girl said to me as we were sitting in the waiting room of the Oncology Department of the General Hospital.

What a pleasant place it is to wait – not at all clinical, like most areas of the hospital, and the staff are trained to be particularly welcoming to all of us who have reasons for going to that particular department. There is also an informality about the atmosphere which is strangely reassuring, and I think the staff should be congratulated on their sheer professionalism and caring attitude, which is very apparent.

Having cancer is not a particularly pleasant illness, and it is wonderful to be diagnosed and cared for by those who can appreciate the reaction of those whose feelings swing from dread to hope.

I looked again at my small acquaintance, whose hair was light brown despite her assertion. She was a most endearing child and I longed to know why she had this misapprehension about her own hair colour. The adults who were with her might have been her mother and grandmother, but they did not offer any explanation about the child's statement.

'Mine's white with a bit of grey,' I said hopefully, thinking, that if she were to compare our hair she might see a difference.

Mine's grey,' she said firmly as they left the waiting room.

I remember reading some time ago that 28 per cent of the male population is colour blind – a fact which I think from my own observation is probably accurate. Both my late beloved husband and my son had the same deficiency and playing snooker with them was always exciting. The inability to see red on green is common.

The female of the species is usually less likely to inherit this genetic condition, so my little grey-haired friend is not likely to be colour blind and will no doubt soon cease to play this little imaginary role.

We all suffer from some form of blindness. Sometimes we are unwilling to see the truth; at other times we fail to see good in someone because of our prejudice; at other times we close our eyes to something that is wrong rather than open them and speak out.

There is so much in the world for us all if we only have the eyes to see it and the heart to love it and the hand to gather it to ourselves.

L M Montgomery

THE TRUE SAINTS ARE REAL, NOT IMAGINED

I WAS grateful to make the acquaintance of two people from Salisbury who were brought along to my cottage by old childhood friends from Aberdeen. It was a very pleasant meeting and reunion and the time passed by very quickly.

Talking to the two new friends from Salisbury, I said how much I had enjoyed seeing the Elisabeth Frink sculpture entitled 'The Walking Madonna' outside the cathedral. It transpired that they lived in Cathedral Close (like Edward Heath, I suppose) and they pass the sculpture every day.

On their return home they sent me a pamphlet with some of the background of the larger-than-life-size bronze figure and I was glad to learn more about it.

Elizabeth Frink's work has been described as 'spare idealism', 'integrity' and 'truthfulness'. I cannot say if that is an accurate description, but 'The Walking Madonna' contains all these attributes and more, for it is a challenging piece of work.

There is nothing of the sweet, rather pious gentle portrayal of Mary which artists and sculptors have been wont to portray. Frink's

Madonna makes her appear as a strong peasant woman walking away from the cathedral as if searching for God outside the place of prayer in which she is usually trapped.

It is a few years since I was in Salisbury, and I have seen many Madonnas in cathedrals in Europe when I have been on the tourist trail. I remember none of them, but 'The Walking Madonna' spoke to me of a real woman, not the demure and sometimes almost passive woman who is usually portrayed.

Perhaps we have done a disservice to many of the saints of history by our failure to see them as real people. Mother Theresa, of blessed and so recent memory, seemed very real to me in life. I wonder how she will be portrayed by the artists and sculptors of today. I hope she will be shown as a woman caring for the poor in the slums of India; that should be her memorial.

Most of us will never achieve saintliness, but we can all go to the aid of others. Helen Keller's life was a constant struggle against disability yet she wrote:

> *I long to accomplish a great and noble task, but it is my chief duty to accomplish small tasks as if they were great and noble.*

QUALITY OF LIFE SHOWN BY A DASH

I HEARD someone speaking on the radio the other day about looking at a tombstone which had the person's name on it and then the dates 1940-1998. The speaker then went on to state that although it is important when one is born and when one dies, it is the bit in between that which is the most important factor. In other words, the dash between the two dates represents a whole life.

It was an early-morning programme and I found myself thinking about the dash in between as I got up and dressed.

Later than morning, before playing a game of bowls, one of my bowling friends said that he had enjoyed life and had worked hard, had good holidays, a happy family life and had been seldom ill.

'You've been lucky,' I said as I sorted out the woods ready for the roll-up. (A roll-up, for the uninitiated to the game of bowls, is when there is no match but bowlers roll-up for enjoyment or for practice.)

'I don't know about luck,' he said. 'I mean, life's what you make it, isn't it?'

I wished that I hadn't started the conversation before the roll-up, but I felt perhaps I ought to mention the people who had worked hard, had a miserable family life and who were dogged by ill health.

I could think of one man crippled by arthritis from an early age who had never been able to get a decent job because of his disability and whose wife left him because she was bored with the limitation which his illness forced upon them both. She took the two children with her, and although he tried desperately hard to get them back, he was unsuccessful.

After I mentioned this as an example of being dealt a bad hand, my bowling colleague said: 'Ah, well, that's life, isn't it?'

The dash on the tombstone which represents the life someone has lived does not indicate the sort of life lived between birth and death. Some people have been dealt a rotten hand and have made the best of it, but the best is sometimes pretty appalling.

I am often asked about life after death, and I frequently reply that for those who have been dealt a wretched hand in this life, surely there will be something better when:

> *It is in giving that we receive, and it is through dying that*
> *we are born to eternal life.*

St Francis of Assisi

HOW IT WILL BE ALL BRIGHT ON THE NIGHT

THE torch which hangs on the wall in the Granary is always on charge. It has a little red light which shows me that the power is going through to the battery and when I have to use it the bulb will shine brightly.

The Granary, which leads into the dining room, was named after my dear mother, known as Gran, who lived with us for the last lovely five years of her life. The Granary is my study and was an addition built in her memory. The only design fault was that I forgot to put an additional light switch on the dining room wall. This meant that I was constantly walking through in the winter darkness and crashing into the table or cracking my shin on one of the dining room chairs.

The dining room table and chairs came with Gran from Aberdeen with a warning that if I did not keep the former well-polished, she would haunt me when she died. So far there have been no supernatural appearances.

Reverting to the torch which Simon gave me two Christmasses ago because of my inability to see in the dark, it has indeed proved a boon. I pick it off its little stand on the wall and light my way through to the farthest switch on the dining room wall. There have been a few occasions when I have forgotten to replace the torch and have not noticed that there is no friendly glow on the wall of the Granary. When retrieved, the torch battery was either flat and showing no signs of life or there was a faint glimmer of complaint from the bulb.

I often feel like my torch. Sometimes my battery is fully charged and I am energy-filled. At other times feel as if the battery is low and I need recharging. Holidays are the best physical recharge. Sometimes, however, we need a spiritual recharge when we need to plug into God. To do this we have to find a quiet place, pray and let His love recharge our flagging spiritual batteries.

> *A jump lead from one fully charged battery to a flat one*
> *will start the engine. Plug a jump lead from you to God*
> *for a surge of spiritual power.*

SEARCHING QUESTIONS OF CHARACTER

THIS is the time of the year when those who have finished university courses and those who are school leavers are looking for employment. Of course, the gap year which has become such a feature of life can intervene, but even those who have back-packed round the world may at this time be looking, albeit reluctantly, for work.

I came across the following in The Times Magazine last month, which I was halfway through before I saw the relevance:

'I thank you for submitting the résumés of the 12 men you have picked for managerial positions in your new organisation. All of them have now taken our tests; we have also arranged personal interviews for each of them with our psychologist and aptitude consultant. It is the staff opinion that most of your nominees are lacking in background, education and vocational aptitude for the type of enterprise you are undertaking.

'Simon Peter is obviously emotionally unstable and given to fits of temper. Andrew has absolutely no qualities of leadership. The two brothers James and John, the sons of Zebedee, place personal interest above company loyalty. Thomas demonstrates a questioning attitude that would tend to undermine morale.

'We feel it is our duty to tell you that Matthew had been blacklisted by the Greater Jerusalem Better Business Bureau. James, the son of Alphaeus, and Thaddaeus definitely have radical leanings, and they both registered a high score on the manic-depressive scale.

'One of the candidates, however, shows great potential. He is a man of ability and resourcefulness, meets people well and has a keen business mind, and has contacts in high places. He is highly motivated and ambitious and responsible. We recommend Judas Iscariot as your controller and right-hand man. All the other profiles are self-explanatory. We wish you every success in your new venture.'

So, with character assessment in mind, may I suggest that job seekers search their souls and consider this saying:

> *What others think of me matters little. What I think of me*
> *matters a little more. What God thinks of me is*
> *all-important.*

EVERY HOUR, ANOTHER GRAIN OF SAND

'WOULD you like to buy me a present?' a friend who was staying with me last month asked. We were walking at the time through the store where once all items cost only sixpence or less.

I can recall my childhood days when a visit to Woollies was the highlight of our week. Clutching the Saturday pennies, warmed by holding them anxiously in my hand, I would fluctuate between the desirability of buying a lead sheep for my model farm and the attraction of purchasing a new eraser shaped like an elephant for my leather pencil case with the initial B emblazoned in gold on the front.

Woolworths, like other stores, has developed over the years, but on the whole a request for a present from that well-known emporium would not normally have sent me into the en désastre scenario. Nevertheless, I did not give her carte blanche, but inquired tentatively what it was she wanted me to buy.

'I want an egg-timer,' she said. I breathed a sign of relief. Mechanical egg-timers which alert one to the duration of time required for some culinary feat were not costly, so I headed towards the electrical counter.

'I would like one with the sand which simply times an egg,' she said.

I stopped in my tracks and turned towards the cookery utensil area. I was rather doubtful about finding such an article, for cookers with built-in timers and handy timing gadgets have largely taken over from the simpler hourglass system of time measurement. However, there was just what she wanted, and I willingly paid the modest amount for her present and we set off for home.

There was a difficulty when we unwrapped the egg-timer, for there were no marks on the glass to indicate the time. However, by simply turning the timer and looking at my watch, we worked out that one could boil an egg for four minutes before the sand ran out.

There is something very primeval about watching the sand run from the top little glass to the bottom. We sometimes say that the sands of time are running out, and, in truth, for all of us this is a fact. It is therefore good sense to spend the time God has given us wisely, for we never know when it may run out.

> *Yesterday is a cancelled cheque, tomorrow is a promissory note, today is cash in hand. Spend it wisely.*

SOLACE AT THE END OF THE DAY

IF I were asked who had made one of the most important contributions to the world in the past 30 years, I would opt for Dame Cicely Saunders. I have never met her, but it has been said of her that she is 'the woman who has changed the face of death'.

Motivated by her faith, Dr Saunders founded St Christopher's Hospice in 1967. Through her pioneering work in London, the hospice movement has mushroomed throughout the British Isles and, indeed, has taken root throughout the world.

For those who have not experienced the loving care and concern of those who endeavour to make the lot of those who are dying bearable, it is perhaps difficult to understand how just entering a hospice can make one aware that the very walls are impregnated with love.

Not the mushy, sentimental love which can be unprofessional, but the skilled, caring and understanding love of those who have dedicated their lives to nursing and looking after those who are terminally ill.

On a recent visit to our local hospice I saw the smiling face of one of our Jurats in an apron, lending a hand with the domestic chores. She told me that it was one of her privileges to help in the hospice.

I have sat with friends who are dying and have been so grateful for the lovely surroundings and beautifully laid out gardens. I know some of the volunteers who are working unceasingly to tend that garden.

The book which is entitled 'Beyond All Pain' is a personal selection by Dr Cicely Saunders, and it contains contributions from patients who found, in hospice, peace at the end of their lives. For those of my readers going through the awful agony of loss, I would commend this anonymous passage by one of those writers:

> *If I should die and leave you here awhile,*
> *Be not like others – sore undone,*
> *Who keep long vigils by the silent dust and weep.*
> *For my sake turn to life and smile,*
> *Nerving thy heart and trembling hands to do*
> *Something to comfort weaker hearts than thine.*
> *Complete those dear unfinished tasks of mine*
> *And I perchance may therein comfort you.*